The Santa Suit

THE SANTA SUIT

MARY KAY ANDREWS

THORNDIKE PRESS
A part of Gale, a Cengage Company

Thorndike Press, a part of Gale, a Cengage Company.

This is a work of fiction. All of the characters, organizations, and events portrayed in this novel are either products of the author's imagination or are used fictitiously.
Thorndike Press® Large Print Core.
The text of this Large Print edition is unabridged.
Other aspects of the book may vary from the original edition.
Set in 16 pt. Plantin.

LIBRARY OF CONGRESS CIP DATA ON FILE.
CATALOGUING IN PUBLICATION FOR THIS BOOK
IS AVAILABLE FROM THE LIBRARY OF CONGRESS.

ISBN-13: 978-1-4328-9124-4 (hardcover alk. paper)

Published in 2021 by arrangement with St. Martin's Publishing Group.

Printed in Mexico
Print Number: 01 Print Year: 2022

For Patti Callahan Henry, aka Peach,
who came along for the ride

Chapter 1

"There it is!" Ivy Perkins pointed at the weather-beaten sign hanging from a dented mailbox nearly obscured by a stand of overgrown dead shrubbery. "Four Roses Farm, Punkin. See it?"

She slowed the Volvo carefully, mindful of the sheets of black ice covering the road.

Punkin barely raised his muzzle from the passenger seat. He'd been dozing since they'd passed through Charlotte, where the steady rain had transitioned to sleet, lulled to sleep by the rhythmic swishing of the windshield wipers and the cheery Christmas music streaming from the Volvo's radio.

The farmhouse driveway was more potholes than paving, and as the car bumped slowly up the narrow stretch, Ivy was adding "new driveway" to the list of home improvements she'd been mentally composing since departing Atlanta in the pre-dawn gloom.

Her heart began to race as the house came into view. There was the front porch she'd been dreaming of. Complete with a row of rockers! Four narrow brick chimneys rose from the corners of the single-story wood-frame house, which meant four fireplaces. Ever since she'd spotted the house in the online real estate listings, she'd been picturing herself seated in front of a cozy fire, in the parlor, sipping hot cider. Okay, to be honest, she pictured herself sipping a good Cabernet. Punkin's bed would be pulled close to the hearth. She would start listening to classical music. And learn to knit. Or crochet. Maybe both.

As she got closer, she noticed the porch seemed to — no, it definitely did have a major sag in the middle that hadn't shown up in the online photographs. And that white paint? Unless the light here was very bad, the color that best came to mind was more curdled buttermilk than white. But all of her online search engine words had very specifically consisted of "old" and "white" and "farmhouse."

She added "paint" to the list of home improvements.

The bumpy ride roused Punkin from his nap. He was sitting up now, alert, tail thumping on the leather upholstery.

She glanced over at him. "What do you think, Punkin? Not really white, but it's definitely old, and since we have almost two acres of land, I'd call that a farmhouse, wouldn't you?"

He thumped his tail again. She would take that as a yes.

Ever since the divorce, she'd taken to talking out loud to the mostly English setter rescue. And not just "good boy" when Punkin completed his business on their walks, or an occasional "who wants a treat?" No, she was having full-on, meaningful conversations with a dog. An exceptionally intelligent, intuitive dog, but still . . .

The driveway ended abruptly in front of a small red structure with more peeling paint. "Look, Punkin!" Ivy squealed. "There it is. Our barn! We have an honest-to-goodness barn!"

Parked directly in front of the barn was a black Jeep. And leaning against the hood of the Jeep was a lanky man dressed in jeans, boots, and a plaid lumberjack-type coat. "Who's this?"

Punkin let out a low-throated *grrr.*

She pulled up in front of the Jeep and got out.

"Hi," she said, eyeing the stranger warily.

He had thick butterscotch-colored hair

sticking out from beneath a baseball cap and the beginnings of a beard, and he didn't seem at all fazed by her presence here. "Hey there," he said lazily, not bothering to move.

"Can I help you?" Ivy said.

"That depends." He was looking at her car, which was packed to the roof with her belongings. Punkin was straining, scratching at the window.

"Depends on what?" she asked impatiently. She would not be intimidated by this intruder.

He held out a ring of keys. "On whether or not you're Ivy Perkins. If you are, I thought you might want the keys to your new house."

"Oh." Ivy looked around the yard, which was decidedly more bedraggled looking than the real estate listing photos. "I was expecting the real estate agent."

"You got him."

"Wait. You're Ezra Wheeler?"

"Correct."

All of her communications with the agent had been conducted through emails or text messages. Ivy had pictured a kindly white-haired gentleman in a bow tie and sweater-vest. Not this . . .

"You were expecting some old geezer, right? Nobody under the age of seventy is named Ezra these days. What can I say? My mom thought she was birthing a sea captain."

"Doesn't matter," Ivy said. "So. This is Four Roses Farm."

"Yup."

"What happened to all the hollyhocks? And the delicate pink roses clambering over the porch railing and the blue hydrangeas?"

"Huh?"

"The pictures from the real estate listings. Everything in those photos looked so lush and green and vibrant." She gestured at the brown, stubbled yard and the colorless, skeletal bushes. "I don't even see one rosebush, let alone four."

He rolled his eyes. "Those photos were taken in the summer. When the house was first listed. And now, it's winter. Win-ter."

Ivy didn't like his patronizing tone. Like he was explaining the seasons to a toddler.

"Also, the Four Roses is a reference to the owners — well, former owners now — Bob and Betty Rae Rose, and their two daughters, Sandi and Emily Rose. Get it? Four Roses."

"I thought the seller's name was James Heywood," Ivy said.

"Yes," Ezra said. "James Heywood's late wife was Sandi Rose Heywood, who inherited this place from her parents, Bob and Betty Rae, who are now deceased. I guess those were roses growing on the porch railing, but since it's December, I'm thinking they're, like, hibernating or something. I'm no gardener, so I can't be sure. Okay? Are we good?" He glanced at his watch, signaling his eagerness to be done with this annoying buyer.

"Fine," Ivy said, holding out her hand for the keys.

"I'll have to unlock the front door for you," Wheeler said. "The lock is old, like the house, and it's kind of tricky."

"Thanks, anyway. But I'm sure I can somehow muddle through a lock all by myself," Ivy said, her tone deliberately frosty.

"Suit yourself," he said, shrugging. "Congrats on the house, by the way. I left you a little housewarming gift on the kitchen counter."

As soon as she opened the Volvo's passenger door, Punkin was off like a shot. He raced to one of the bushes bordering the porch and christened it before returning to Ivy's side as she dragged a suitcase up the porch steps.

The first thing she noticed about the

porch itself was that the worn floorboards seemed to bounce slightly with every step she took. Did that mean she had foundation issues? She sighed and for the first time felt a twinge of regret that she hadn't actually toured the 106-year-old farmhouse in person before making her offer.

There were six keys on the ring Ezra Wheeler had handed her, none of which was labeled. Ivy tried four different keys until she finally managed to fit a black, old-timey-looking skeleton key into the front door lock. She held the egg-shaped doorknob firmly in her left hand and managed to make a quarter turn with the key. She turned the knob, but the door didn't budge. She pushed against the doorframe, sending a shower of pale blue paint flakes down the front of her jeans. Nothing.

Ivy tried jiggling the lock and jiggling the door. She walked completely around the house, trying keys in four more doors, to no avail. She peered in a window at the back of the house, into the kitchen, but the glass was wavy and blackened with grime, so she only got a glimpse of a kitchen sink and a small wooden table and chairs.

"Come on, Punkin," she said, heading back around to the front of the house. She pulled her phone from her jacket pocket.

"Looks like we're gonna give Ezra a call and admit defeat."

Five minutes later, the Jeep was jouncing down the driveway.

"That didn't take long," Ivy said as he joined her on the front porch.

"I was just waiting down at the cross-roads," he said, giving her a sheepish grin. "And I did try to warn you. That lock really is the dickens to open."

He grasped the doorknob firmly, inserted the lock into the key, jiggled it a moment, then slowly turned the key to the left. As the tumblers finally clicked, he rammed his shoulder against the door, muscling it open.

"You turn it to the left?" Ivy was indig-nant. "You could have told me that."

"Would you have believed me?" He picked up her suitcase and gestured for her to enter the house.

Ivy paused. She'd been waiting for this moment for nine months. This day, the day she took possession of her dream farm-house, was no accident. It was intentional. Nine months ago, to the day, her divorce from Kyle had been final.

She'd made an intentional decision to start a new life in a new town in a new state, but in an old house.

Ivy wasn't sure she wanted to start her new life in the company of this stranger, no matter how helpful he was trying to be.

Ezra looked back at her, puzzled. "Aren't you coming in? I thought I'd show you the house."

She took a deep breath and stepped over the threshold with Punkin close behind.

Ivy looked around the living area. The old pine floors were scarred but beautiful to her. The fireplace, with an oak mantelpiece and mottled tile surround, was just the same as in the listing photos.

She lifted a dusty sheet from what turned out to be a large, lumpy plaid sofa straight out of *The Brady Bunch.*

"What's with all this?" she asked, gesturing at the matching plaid recliner. "There was nothing in the contract about me buying the place furnished."

"Yeah, about that," Ezra said, looking sheepish. "James's kids only wanted a couple of pieces of their granddad's furniture, so he decided at the last minute to leave it all for the buyer."

"You mean he decided to dump all this old crap on me," Ivy said, her voice sounding harsher than she'd intended.

Ezra winced.

"Never mind," she said quickly. "I've been up since four and it's been a long day already. It's just that my movers will be here Monday with all my stuff."

"I get it," Ezra said. "I did tell James you probably wouldn't want any of this. I can get a truck and a couple guys over here in the next couple of days, and if you want, it can all be donated to charity."

She walked into the kitchen. The cabinets were dated, but serviceable. The stove and refrigerator were a recent vintage. But all of it, she decided, would eventually have to go.

"Everything works," Ezra said quickly. "I had the power changed over to your name, like you asked, and the water's hooked up too."

"Thanks for that," Ivy said. Her mind was racing with additions to her list of improvements.

He trailed her into the hallway off the living room. "The master bedroom's at the back here," he volunteered.

She nodded and opened the door. The bedroom was larger than she'd expected. The furniture was ugly, but serviceable.

"Okay," she said quietly. "Okay."

"Where were you expecting to sleep until your moving truck arrives?" Ezra asked.

"I've got a sleeping bag in the car," Ivy

said. She sat on the edge of the bed, and the springs wheezed loudly. "But I guess this'll do until my own bed gets here."

"Great," Ezra said, sounding relieved. "Can I help you unload your car?"

She considered rejecting the offer. But she was tired, and the car was full, and she had a lot to do before the movers arrived.

"That'd be great," she said.

Ezra Wheeler bent down and peered into the back of the Volvo, and Ivy was surprised to find herself checking him out. Cute butt. He lifted out a large cardboard carton that had a row of ventilation holes cut in the sides. A series of muffled peeps erupted.

"What the . . . ?"

Peep. Peep. Peeppeepeeeep . . .

She took the box from his arms. "These are the girls." She lifted the box top, and the four fluffy chicks began scuttling around the straw she'd arranged in their makeshift carrier.

"Chickens? You brought chickens? From Atlanta?"

"Yes," she said, feeling weirdly self-conscious. "I did. They'll stay in the house where it's warm for now, and then I'll rig up a coop for them in the barn."

Ezra brought in two more loads of her

belongings while she settled the box of chicks in a corner of the kitchen, which, for now, seemed like the warmest place in the noticeably chilly house.

"I think this is all of it," he said, bringing in an armload of her hanging clothes.

"Let's take that into my bedroom," Ivy said, leading him down the hall.

She opened the closet door and was startled by the sight of a tightly packed row of clothing: dresses, skirts, men's shirts, and pants.

"Dammit," she muttered. She grabbed a bunch of coat hangers and began tossing clothing onto the floor. Ezra followed her lead, and five minutes later the closet had been cleaned out.

Ivy stood with her hands on her hips, surveying the space. Like all the rooms in the house, the bedroom and the closet had ten-foot ceilings. There were two shelves above the clothes rod, and she spotted a box on the top shelf. She stood on her tiptoes but still couldn't reach it.

"I can get it." Ezra easily plucked the box off the shelf and showed it to her.

The box was wrapped in vintage Christmas wrapping paper featuring dancing elves and candy canes and Christmas trees, and it was tied with red satin ribbon.

Ivy placed the box on the bed, untied the ribbon, and opened the box. She lifted aside layers of yellowing tissue paper to reveal a folded red velvet jacket with a white fur collar.

She removed the jacket from the box, laying it on top of the chenille bedspread. Beneath it was a pair of trousers, in the same fabric, with white fur trimmings on the cuffs. Beneath that was a pair of soft black leather boots with large brass buckles.

"It's a Santa suit," Ivy whispered. But this wasn't just any suit. It was a beautifully tailored, luxurious garment — nothing like the fairly plain furnishings and clothing she'd encountered in the rest of the farmhouse.

She stroked the fabric, which was real velvet, with real white fur trim. The jacket was lined in satin, and it fastened with a hidden buttoned placket. There was a belt of shiny, if somewhat cracked, black patent leather, with a large brass buckle. When she lifted the boots, she discovered the hat made of matching red velvet with a satin lining, fur trim, and a white pom-pom.

"Ohhh," she said softly.

"Well damn," Ezra said. "That must be Big Bob's Santa suit."

He saw her puzzled expression.

"The previous owner? According to what I've been told by the locals, Bob Rose *was* Santa Claus in these mountains." Ezra returned to the closet, running his hands over the shelves. "Huh. Looks like it's not here."

"What? Rudolph? The sleigh?"

"Mrs. Santa's costume. According to my broker, Betty Rae Rose had an outfit she'd wear that matched Bob's outfit." He shrugged. "Maybe one of the grandkids decided they wanted it."

"Too bad they didn't decide to take the rest of this junk," Ivy said, pointing at the pile of clothing in the corner of the bedroom, where Punkin had already made himself a nest.

"I'll have my guys haul off anything you don't want," Ezra promised, looking at his watch again. "Sorry, I'd better go."

"Big date?" He wasn't wearing a wedding ring, and much to her own annoyance, she'd been wondering about his marital status.

"Seeing a client about a potential new listing," he said. "Divorce. It's the gift that keeps giving." He paused at the front door. "Welcome home, by the way."

Chapter 2

As darkness fell on Four Roses Farm, the little farmhouse took on a more noticeable chill. Ivy paused in her unpacking and bundled up, donning a bulky sweater, a knit scarf, and two pairs of socks, as she searched the house for a thermostat for the heater, but came up short.

She dashed out to the side porch and brought in an armload of logs and stacked it in the fireplace in the living room, adding a handful of dried-out pine cones she salvaged from a dusty arrangement on the mantel, and some crumpled up sheets of newspaper with a 1998 dateline she'd found lining the shelves of the pantry.

"Here goes nothing," she told Punkin, who was watching her progress while lolling near the hearth. She did a little happy dance when the tiny flame caught, then flickered, then blazed. "Now for some supper."

The setter's ears pricked up and he followed her into the kitchen, where, for the first time, she noticed the large gift bag on the counter. She lifted out a very good bottle of red wine and a gaily decorated round tin full of cookies. The handwritten gift label taped to the lid said: MAMA W'S OATMEAL CHOCOLATE CHIP COOKIES. DEFINITELY NOT LOW-CAL. OR GLUTEN-FREE.

"It's the thought that counts, right?" she asked Punkin, pushing the cookie tin aside. There was a small pamphlet — *New Homeowner's Checklist — Courtesy of Carolina Countryside Realty and Ezra Wheeler* — clipped to the side of the gift bag.

Ivy read down the items, convinced she'd already taken care of all the red tape involved in moving. Her father had been an engineer, and Ivy had been raised to be detail oriented. She'd already filled out all the change-of-address forms, applied for a North Carolina registration and license tag for the Volvo, and even ordered a driver's handbook in preparation for applying for a driver's license in her new state.

Some of the actions on the list — like enrolling children in school — didn't apply to Ivy. But there were a couple items she'd overlooked, at the end of the checklist. "Register to vote." "Apply for homestead exemption." "Register pets and obtain rabies tags."

"Paperwork," she muttered with a sigh. "Endless paperwork."

Punkin just stared up at her, thumping his tail on the floor.

"Never mind that. Let's check on our girls." The chicks were snuggled into a corner of their cardboard carrier in a pile of straw. But the kitchen was cold, even colder than the rest of the house, so she carried their box into the living room and set it on a table near the hearth. Punkin pushed his muzzle up against the box and sniffed, wagging his tail.

"I know you're supposed to be a bird dog," Ivy chided. "But these girls are part of our family now, so you leave them alone."

Dinner was high protein kibble for Punkin and for her, cheese and crackers, washed down with some of the excellent Cabernet she'd been gifted from Ezra Wheeler. She rinsed off her plate and the jelly jar she'd used as a wineglass and vowed to call him in the morning to thank him for the housewarming gift — and to inquire about the status of her new home's heating system.

She spent the rest of the evening scrubbing the kitchen floor, counters, and cabinets before unpacking the boxes of kitchen equipment she'd loaded into her car.

When she looked up, it was after nine. "C'mon, Punkin," she said. "It's past our bedtime."

The bedroom was even colder than the kitchen, and the cause, she quickly discovered, was a small missing pane of glass in the window across from the bed. As she ripped a piece of cardboard from one of her packing boxes and taped it over the window, she observed that all the windowpanes were loose and drafty. Probably every window in the house was in similar condition. She ruefully added new windows to the growing list of home repairs she'd been compiling ever since she'd pulled into the driveway at Four Roses Farm.

Punkin had already arranged himself across the foot of her bed, which was still draped with the red Santa suit. Surely, Ivy thought, Santa Bob's family would want this sentimental family heirloom. After she shooed Punkin off the bed and onto his own fleece-lined dog bed, she placed the hat, boots, and trousers in the box where she'd found them. But as she was smoothing and folding the jacket, she felt something in one of the hidden pockets.

She unfolded a sheet of deeply creased blue-lined school notebook paper:

Dear Santa: I have been a very good girl this year. But I am sad becuz my mama is sad. If you could bring my daddy home from the war my mama would smile again and we would be happy and I would also like a puppy, but if you only bring me one thing, that's okay. Please, Santa, bring my daddy home safe. His name is Everett and he has red hair, just like me. Your friend, Carlette.

Tears pricked at Ivy's eyes as she ran a fingertip over the note's childish scrawl. She added the Santa jacket to the box and set it on top of the dresser. It was too cold in the room for pajamas, so she spread her sleeping bag on top of the bedspread, topped it with a colorful patchwork quilt she'd found in the hall linen closet, and crawled, fully dressed, beneath the covers. She'd just turned off the lamp on the nightstand when Punkin leaped onto the bed.

"All right," she said, stroking the silky fur of his ears. "Just this once. But tomorrow you sleep in your own bed. Understand?" The dog licked Ivy's neck and burrowed in beside her.

Punkin was snoring softly within minutes, but as tired as she was, Ivy's brain worriedly ticked away at her growing to-do list.

She'd been excited with what she thought of as the "sexy stuff" like installing a new kitchen, updating bathrooms, and planting her first real garden at the Four Roses farmhouse. But she hadn't counted on the mundane, potentially budget-busting stuff that hadn't turned up in the inspection report — but would still need immediate attention — the sagging porch, pothole-pocked driveway, and drafty windows.

In her mind, she ticked off the number of windows in the house. There were four double windows in this bedroom alone. Two or three in the guest bedroom? And all those living room windows that faced on to the front porch? If she kept dwelling on the mounting cost of renovations and her dwindling bank account, she'd never get to sleep.

She yawned and rolled over, catching sight of the Santa suit in the dimly lit room. She began reconsidering the note she'd discovered in the jacket pocket. Who was Carlette, she wondered, and her daddy? And had Santa brought him safely home?

Her thoughts drifted to her own childhood, when she'd a similarly impossible request to the mall Santa she'd visited with her grandmother. Somewhere, maybe in the boxes the movers would bring on Monday, she had a photo that documented that visit.

Little Ivy Perkins, age six, with the unfortunate bangs her grandmother had insisted upon styling herself, dressed in an itchy green and white smocked dress with clown-like puffed sleeves.

In the photo, her eyes looked sorrowfully upon the mall Santa, an irritable man with halitosis, who'd laughed uncomfortably at her one and only request. "We'll see," he'd said, and then he'd shoved her into the waiting arms of a helper elf who'd given her a broken candy cane and a coloring book.

After her grandmother shelled out the $5.99 for the photo, they'd had dinner at the mall's food court. Ivy had been allowed to order the most exotic dish she'd ever seen, *kung pao* chicken, and egg rolls from a steam table. Nana had coffee and a slice of pie.

"What did you ask Santa to bring you for Christmas?" Nana asked.

"It's a secret," Ivy had whispered, toying with the syrupy orange chicken.

Her grandmother smiled and patted her hand. "Well, you've been a very good girl, so I'm sure whatever it is, Santa will do his best to get it for you."

She got violently carsick on the way home, and the hated green and white dress had to be thrown away.

On Christmas morning, when her father woke her up and escorted her downstairs to the Christmas tree, Ivy found an American Girl doll with a trunk full of clothes. In between unwrapping gifts, Ivy kept peering toward the front door, hoping and praying that between Mall Santa and Baby Jesus, who was cradled in her grandmother's china manger scene, her one wish would be granted.

Finally, at dinnertime, she'd figured it out. Nana's table was set with the good damask cloth and real napkins and the plates with the tiny blue flowers and gold edging that only came out for the holidays. There were candles in the silver candlesticks. But only three plates were set at the table.

"When is Mama coming home?"

Her father exchanged a troubled glance with Nana.

"As soon as she's better," Nana said.

It was the last time Ivy had trusted Santa Claus.

Chapter 3

She called Ezra Wheeler first thing in the morning. "There's no heat," she announced. "My inspection report said the house had central heating."

"Good morning to you too," he said. "The furnace works just fine. But remember, the house has been closed up for months and months."

"I couldn't even find a thermostat," she groused. She was standing in the kitchen, in an admittedly foul mood because she hadn't packed her coffeemaker.

"It's at the end of the hallway."

"Oh." Her voice was meek. She hadn't been able to get the Santa note out of her mind. "Thanks. You don't happen to have the seller's phone number, do you? I have a couple of questions for him."

"As a matter of fact, James is leaving town this morning, but he asked if it would be okay if he stopped by this morning to pick up a family photo album," Ezra said.

"That'd be fine."

"Also, I can have a truck there tomorrow, to pick up the furniture you want donated."

"Great. Thanks. And thanks for the wine and the cookies."

James Heywood retrieved the photo album from the bookshelf in the back bedroom, and then he showed Ivy where the thermostat was located.

"My in-laws were pretty thrifty people," he explained. "They didn't have the central heat installed here until the eighties."

Ivy was grateful for the stream of warm air now flowing through the floor vents.

"Did Ezra happen to mention the Santa suit I found?" she asked.

"Oh yeah. I'd forgotten all about that. Feel free to donate it with the rest of the old clothes and stuff."

"You don't want it? I assumed it was a family heirloom."

"I guess I'm not very sentimental. The suit belonged to my father-in-law. Big Bob, that's what everyone in town called him, and Betty Rae, they played Santa and Mrs. Claus all over this part of the North Carolina mountains, at Atkins Department Store, before they closed, and then the VFW and the Elks Lodge, and at the children's home."

Ivy handed him the note. "The thing is, I found this in the jacket pocket of the Santa suit. And I was wondering who Carlette was? And her father."

His face softened as he read the Santa note. "Oh, wow. That's so sad. I guess maybe this little girl's daddy was in Vietnam? But I have no idea who these people might be. I didn't grow up here. My wife was the local."

"Maybe she knew the family?"

James's smile faded. "I wish I could ask her. Sandi died two years ago. Breast cancer. She never would sell the house after her parents passed. But now, she's gone and my kids have no interest in living in this 'hick town,' as they call it."

"To each his own," Ivy said lightly as she showed him to the front door.

The chicks were awake now and peeping loudly from their cardboard box.

"Are those chickens?" James asked, looking amused.

"Yep." She left it at that.

"Can I ask you a question?"

"You mean, what's a nice, single, big-city girl like me doing in a hick town like Tarburton?"

He laughed. “Something like that.”

She shrugged. “I’m not entirely sure I know myself. I guess I was ready for a change.”

“Big change, coming from Atlanta to a burg with a population of fifteen hundred people.”

“Blame it on the chickens,” Ivy said.

“Huh?”

“When I was a little girl, my great-aunt lived way out in the country in a little farmhouse. And she had chickens. They’d come and sit on your lap and eat out of your hand. You can’t keep chickens in just any old place, you know. Turns out, there are all kinds of rules. So, when I started house hunting, I decided to find a place where I could keep chickens.”

James gazed out the window. “Betty Rae, my mother-in-law, used to keep chickens, back in the day. There might still be an old coop somewhere out back.”

“It’s on my list of things to check out,” Ivy said. “Thanks again for stopping by.”

He took one last, long, wistful look around the living room. “There are a lot of good memories in this old house. Bob and Betty Rae were wonderful folks. They were mainstays in this community for a lot of years. I hope you'll love this place as much as they did."

She spent the next hour boxing up what seemed like several generations of the Rose family's clothing to donate to charity. But she didn't have the heart to donate the Santa suit. It had been special to Bob and Betty Rae Rose, and maybe someday it would be special to someone again. In the meantime, there was no harm in keeping it right here at their former homeplace.

"Okay, Punkin," Ivy said, rousting the dog from the sun-soaked spot he'd claimed by the front window. "I'm gonna walk into town to do some paperwork and maybe rustle up some caffeine. You stay here and guard the chickens, okay?"

Punkin raised his muzzle, sniffed the air, and went right back to sleep.

It was just after eleven, and the air was cold and crisp, with what her father called bluebird skies. Ivy scuffed along through the fallen leaves on the narrow two-lane blacktop road into town, waving at the occasional truck or car that slowed, then passed by. As she walked, her thoughts returned to the poignant note tucked in the pocket of the Santa suit.

Maybe, while she was in town, she could

find out more about the identity of the note's author.

Tarburton was clearly a town that got behind Christmas. Display windows in the shops around the square were decked out for the holidays, all the utility poles wore large evergreen wreaths with perky red bows, and in the center of the square itself was a towering Fraser fir glittering with oversized white, silver, and gold ornaments and lights.

Ivy wandered around the business district until she spotted a café called The Coffee Cup.

Every booth in the café was occupied, but she slid onto an empty stool at the counter right next to the cash register. The walls were egg yolk yellow and the countertop was yellow Formica and the room buzzed with dozens of conversations.

"Coffee?" The waitress placed a thick china mug before her and started to pour before Ivy had time to answer.

"You know what you want to eat?" The waitress looked to be about Ivy's age, with white blond hair swept into a high ponytail and dark penciled-on eyebrows.

"Could I see a menu?"

The waitress slid a laminated sheet of paper in front of Ivy. "You must be new in town, huh?"

Ivy scanned the menu. "Yes, I just moved in." She was trying to decide between a club sandwich and a hot roast beef sandwich.

"The special's good today. Pork chop, baked apples, and collard greens," the waitress said, pointing to a piece of paper clipped to the menu. "Whereabouts did you move to? If you don't mind my asking."

"I'll have the special, then," Ivy said. "Do you know Four Roses Farm?"

"You mean the Christmas house? Bob and Betty Rae's old place? I didn't even know it was for sale."

"That's the one," Ivy said. "Did you happen to know the Roses? I found this old Santa suit, and there's a note in the pocket I'm wondering about. . . ."

"You want that chop fried or baked?" the waitress asked.

"Baked."

"Corn bread or biscuit?"

"Biscuit."

"Got it." The waitress walked away, scribbling on her order pad.

Ivy sipped her coffee and half listened to the buzz of conversation surrounding her. Ten minutes later, the waitress slid a heaping plate in front of her. "Thanks," Ivy said.

"Are y'all gonna start lighting up the

Christmas house again this year?" the waitress asked, tucking Ivy's check under the edge of the plate.

Ivy shook her head. There was no "y'all" at the farmhouse, unless you included Punkin, but she knew from experience that he was useless at chores that required opposable thumbs.

"Afraid not," she said, taking a bite of pork chop. "I just moved in, and there's so much to do, because the house hasn't been lived in —"

"Well, that's a damn shame," the waitress said, cutting her off. She flounced off to the far end of the counter. As Ivy ate her lunch she saw the waitress leaning across the counter, conversing with another diner in a loud whisper, her eyes shooting daggers in Ivy's direction.

She hurriedly finished her lunch and set off across the square to finish her errands.

At the county courthouse, a small but stately white Greek Revival building, she stopped at the animal control office and applied for Punkin's dog tag and presented his vet records for rabies certification. Then she found the clerk's office and filled out the paperwork to change her voter registration and file for homestead exemption.

"So, you're the lady who bought Four Roses, huh?" asked the clerk as he looked over the documents she'd just filled out. He was an older man who looked to be in his early sixties. The name badge pinned to his carefully starched shirt read: "Herman Schoonover."

"Welcome to Tarburton."

She waited to be asked about the Christmas lights, but he busied himself typing something into his computer.

"Thanks," she said. "Did you know the Rose family?"

"Oh, sure," he said. "Everybody knew Bob and Betty Rae, rest their souls. They were the salt of the earth. They sure made Christmas special for the folks in this town."

"I understand Mr. Rose used to play Santa Claus," Ivy said.

"That's right. Every kid who grew up in these parts sat on Santa Bob's lap over the years, my own kids and grandkids included."

"I know it's a long shot," Ivy said. "But I'm looking for a father and daughter who I think used to live around here. The father's name is Everett, and the daughter's name was Carlette. And I think the father must have served in the military. Probably Vietnam?"

"Last name?"

"I'm hoping you can tell me."

Mr. Schoonover scratched his nose while he thought about it. "No, those names don't ring a bell, but I didn't move to town until the mid-eighties. Which makes me a newcomer to some folks."

"Like me," Ivy said, handing him her paperwork.

"Any special reason you're looking for these folks?" he asked.

Ivy hesitated. It sounded far-fetched, even to her. "I found a note. In the pocket of Mr. Rose's Santa suit, from this little girl named Carlette, asking Santa to bring her father home safely. From the war. It . . . touched me."

"Wish I could help you," Mr. Schoonover said. He puffed out his chest a little. "I'm an old Navy man myself." He tapped some keys on his computer, nodded, and looked up. "Okay. You're all squared away here. Have yourself a good Christmas, you hear?"

It had started to warm up while she was in the courthouse, so Ivy decided to check out the town square. There was a fountain in the middle, near the soldier's memorial statue, and she'd noticed it had a special spigot, close to the ground, for dogs. Now that Punkin was a legal resident, she'd bring him along on her next visit to town.

She sat on a bench near the memorial, enjoying the feel of the winter sun on her face as she took inventory of the shops around the square. From here she spotted a hardware store and a gift shop, the café where she'd had lunch, a candy shop, and a florist.

"Hi!"

The young woman stood a few feet away. She was in her early twenties, Ivy thought, with dark, expressive eyes, long, wavy brown hair, and a shy smile, and she looked vaguely familiar.

"Hi," Ivy said.

"Don't think I'm weird, but I work in the clerk's office, and I couldn't help but overhear you just now, asking Mr. Schoonover about someone named Carlette? My name's Phoebe Huddleston, by the way."

"Hi, Phoebe, I'm Ivy Perkins. You don't seem too weird to me. What's up?"

"The thing is, my mom's best friend's name, growing up, was Carlette. She almost named me that, but anyway, it's not a real common name, so I thought —"

"Maybe your mom knew Carlette? And her family?" Ivy asked eagerly.

"Mom lives over in Rockdale, but I'm going over there this weekend, so I could ask, if you want. Or maybe you could come with me and ask her yourself. She loves having company."

Ivy thought about everything she needed to accomplish at Four Roses Farm before the moving truck with her belongings arrived. There were more closets and cupboards to be emptied, the broken window in her bedroom needed to be replaced, and she wanted to walk her new property and check out the old chicken coop. Her to-do list was long and time was short.

But. The prospect of discovering the fate of Carlette's father was irresistible. She took out a scrap of paper and scribbled her phone number on it. "Here's how to reach me. I would love to meet your mom and ask about Carlette."

CHAPTER 4

Ivy stood back from the fireplace wall to admire her progress. She'd spent the morning painting the parlor. The color she'd chosen was a soft blue-gray-green that seemed to change as the light shifted in the room. It was the exact color — or so she hoped — of the eggs her Araucana chicks would lay, eventually.

She'd made another surprise discovery too, while getting ready to paint the front doorframe. A small wooden carved object with Hebrew lettering, which had been screwed to the right side of the doorframe.

"Huh." It looked to be a mezuzah. It was yet another puzzle, finding a traditional symbol of the Jewish faith — at a home owned by a family known far and wide for their embrace of all things Christmas.

She heard the sound of a vehicle in the driveway. Punkin heard it too and gave a short, sharp bark. When she looked out the window she saw a large box truck parked there, and Ezra Wheeler and a helper were wheeling a furniture dolly onto the porch.

"Hi!" she said, opening the front door. "I thought you'd call to let me know you were coming?"

"No time," Ezra said. He gestured to the other man, who was burly and bald. "Jake, meet Ivy. She's the one I told you about."

Jake looked around the living room. Ivy had managed to shove most of the furniture into a corner, with the exception of the bulky sofa.

"You're donating all this to the community thrift store? What are you going to sit on?"

"My own furniture should be here Monday," Ivy said. "Until then, I've got a chair and a little table in the kitchen. I don't need more than that."

"Okay," Jake said. "You're the boss."

Two hours later, all the rooms in the house were bare, with the exception of a mattress in Ivy's bedroom and the wooden table and chair in the kitchen.

The men's voices echoed in the high-ceilinged living room as they moved the last item, a heavy wooden footlocker. As they rolled the furniture dolly over the front doorjamb, the chest slipped off the dolly and fell, spilling papers and file folders all over the floor.

"Sorry," Jake said, examining a gash in the wooden floor.

Ivy knelt down, gathering up the papers. There were old newspaper clippings, greeting cards, photographs, and letters. So many letters, all addressed simply "SANTA, Tarburton, NC."

"Look at this!" she exclaimed, holding up a black-and-white photo of the jolly old elf himself, seated on an elaborately tufted chair, holding a little girl in his lap.

"Yup, that's Santa Bob," Jake said, examining the photo.

Ivy read the hand-lettering on the back. "Atkins Dept. Store, 1962. Darlene Meyers." She picked up another photo, this one of Mr. and Mrs. Claus, standing on a parade float, waving to bystanders. "Christmas Parade 1990."

She scooped up a handful of letters and replaced them in a folder marked SANTA LETTERS and showed them to Ezra. "Some of these postmarks go back to the 1960s. Looks like Big Bob kept every letter from every child he ever received."

Jake shifted from one foot to the other, looking down at the trunk. "Uh, sorry to break up this little sentimental journey, y'all, but I gotta get this truck back."

Ivy sighed. "It's just a shame to throw away this stuff. I wonder if the local historical society would want any of it."

"We could just leave the trunk here," Jake said hopefully.

"Yes, please," she said, laughing. "Sorry for the change of heart."

While Jake went to stow the furniture dolly, Ezra looked around the now-bare room. The only remaining item, with the exception of the ladder, was Punkin's bed, near the hearth.

"I like the paint job," he said. His voice echoed in the high-ceilinged room. "But what happened to the chicks?"

"I moved them out to the kitchen where they get the morning sun, then I'll bring them back here to the living room later in the afternoon."

"Where'll you put your Christmas tree?" he asked.

"I wasn't planning on getting a tree this year," Ivy said. "I mean, it's just me and Punkin. Anyway, my ex got all our Christmas decorations in the divorce settlement."

"All of them? That kind of sucks, doesn't it?"

Ivy shrugged. "Most of them were from his family. I don't mind. Decorating for

Christmas isn't really a priority for me this year what with all I need to do around here."

"Like what?"

She ticked off the items on her list. "Number one is replace the missing pane of glass in the bedroom window. I'm afraid I'll eventually have to replace or reglaze all these drafty old windows. But in the meantime, there's another missing pane in the back bedroom window, and then my bathroom sink is stopped up, and I want to replace that front door lock because it really is too tricky. And then there's the chicken coop . . ."

"I might know a guy," Ezra said. A horn honked from the driveway. "Okay, I'd better go."

Her new friend, Phoebe, called just as Ivy was washing the last traces of paint from her hands and arms.

"Hey, Ivy. My mom said she'd love to talk to you about her friend Carlette. I'm going over there this afternoon, and you could go with me if you want."

"I'd love that," Ivy said.

"I'll pick you up at four."

Sally Huddleston read the Santa letter out

loud, then folded it and handed it back to Ivy.

"This brings back so many memories," she said, sighing. "Carlette and her mama lived across the street from my family, growing up on Spruce Street. I believe that house belonged to Mr. Jones's parents, and they were staying there while Mr. Jones was off in Vietnam."

"Jones?" Ivy said eagerly. "That was her last name?"

"Yes." Mrs. Huddleston nodded. "I know her daddy's name was Everett, and her mama's name was something with a *D.* Debra? Or Donna? Of course, I always just called her Mrs. J. I asked my own mother once why Mrs. J. hardly ever smiled or laughed, and she said it was because of the war."

"Do you know how to reach Carlette now?" Ivy asked. "Do you know if her father did make it back from Vietnam?"

"No, honey," Mrs. Huddleston said sadly. "I honestly don't know if he did. They moved away, I think it was right before we started third grade. Somewhere in South Carolina where Mrs. J had family of her own. We were both real tore up about it, because up until then, we were inseparable. We were pen pals for a while, but then I guess one of us quit writing."

"Did you save any of her letters?"

"I did," Mrs. Huddleston said. "Saved 'em up in a Whitman's Sampler candy box, but who knows what happened to that? I wish I had more answers to give you."

Ivy's shoulder sagged a little, and Mrs. Huddleston gave her knee a sympathetic pat. "How are you liking Four Roses Farm? I sure hope you're going to keep up Bob and Betty Rae's tradition."

"Dressing up as Santa and Mrs. Claus?" Ivy laughed. "I don't think so."

"No, no. I mean, getting the place all lit up for Christmas. My gosh, the two of them worked on those decorations year-round. Lights everywhere! My husband used to say you could probably see Bob's lights from outer space."

"Daddy used to load all of us up in the van and take us out to the farmhouse to see all the lights," Phoebe put in. "Everybody in town did the same thing."

"A couple of people have told me about that, but Christmas lights aren't really my thing," Ivy said apologetically. "I was just telling my real estate agent, Ezra, I probably won't even get a tree."

"Oh," Mrs. Huddleston said. "That's a shame. I think everybody needs a little

Christmas spirit in these times, don't you?"

"Maybe next year," Ivy said vaguely. "And speaking of time, I've probably taken up enough of yours for today."

"Right," Phoebe said, catching Ivy's signal. "I'll see you tomorrow, Mom."

"Wait!" Mrs. Huddleston said, jumping to her feet. "You didn't even taste my cake yet. And I baked it special for you, Ivy. I'll just wrap it up for you. Cake to go!"

"You shouldn't have," Ivy said. "I don't really eat a lot of sweets. . . ."

But Mrs. Huddleston was already bustling around out in the kitchen.

"Wait'll you taste this cake," Phoebe said. "I'm on a strict diet, but I promise you will go crazy when you taste it!"

"Here we are!" Mrs. Huddleston said, triumphantly thrusting a foil-wrapped parcel into Ivy's hands. "My S'mores Butterscotch Caramel Choco Dump Cake!"

"Yum!" Ivy said, feeling queasy. "Can't wait!"

"And I just now remembered Carlette's mama's name. It was Diana. Diana Jones."

CHAPTER 5

Sunday morning dawned colder, but clear. Ivy pulled on jeans, boots, and her warmest jacket. "C'mon, Punkin!" she called. "Let's go walk the back forty!"

The dog cast a baleful eye in her direction. He was content by the fire she'd built.

"Oh, come on. It'll be fun. You can chase some squirrels."

Woodsmoke curled through the air, and dead grass and acorns crunched beneath her boots as she toured the property. In a sunny patch near the back porch she found what had surely been a beloved rose garden, but now the bushes looked stunted and unloved. Someday, Ivy thought, she would have roses in this spot: pink, yellow, white, and coral roses.

Oak trees, evergreens, and tall pines were dotted around the landscape. A huge camellia bush was planted a few yards from the back porch and she leaned in and plucked a delicate pink blossom, tucking it behind one ear. There were towering holly bushes too, bristling with clusters of fat red berries that contrasted with their gleaming leaves.

"All mine," Ivy whispered, turning to Punkin. But the dog was racing and romping around the property, chasing squirrels and having the time of his life.

Not far from the camellia bush she found the remains of a vegetable garden. Dried cornstalks and forlorn tomato cages promised that this had once been fertile ground. Nearby was a rustic shed that covered an ancient-looking tractor and an assortment of rusty rakes, shovels, and hoes. Just beyond the shed she found the chicken coop.

Rather, what was left of it. One side of the coop seemed to have collapsed under the weight of a tin roof, and a spindly tree had taken up root inside the coop, pushing through a hole in the roof.

"So . . . chicken coop rebuild," Ivy said aloud. Her bargain farmhouse was seeming like less and less of a good buy every day. According to what she'd read online, her chicks would probably outgrow their cardboard crate within two or three weeks. They needed a real coop, with room to run around in, perches to sleep on, and nesting boxes. She could already feel her bank account shrinking.

She was walking back toward the house when she heard what sounded like hammering — coming from the house.

"Punkin! Here, boy. Punkin!" She whistled, and the dog raced back to her side, tail wagging, tongue lolling. His sleek white coat was dotted with burrs and leaves and mud and he looked supremely happy.

Ivy spotted the black Jeep in the driveway as she rounded the side of the house. There was a man on the front porch, and he seemed intent on hammering something into her door.

"Hello?"

Ezra Wheeler looked up from his project. He wore a leather tool belt around his waist and had a screwdriver jammed beneath the front doorknob.

"Oh hey," he said easily. "I wondered where you'd gotten to."

"What exactly are you doing?" Ivy demanded.

"You mentioned the lock needed to be replaced. I had some time to kill today, so I thought I'd stop by and take a look. The screws on this doorknob are stripped. Good thing I picked up a new knob, just in case."

"You bought me a new lock and now you're installing it? Is that the kind of thing you do for all your clients?"

He shrugged. "Just the ones who buy a house online without ever actually seeing what the property looks like. Guess I'm feeling a little guilty that you got sucked into this big of a fixer-upper."

"Oh, I get it," Ivy said. "You feel sorry for the poor dumb city girl. But I assure you, I entered into this transaction fully aware of what I was buying."

"No!" Ezra protested. "Yesterday, you asked if I knew a handyman. I do. Me. Look, why do you want to make a whole big deal of this?"

Ivy looked at him. His warm brown eyes seemed earnest.

"I'm just not used to strangers doing me favors," she admitted. "First you moved out all that old furniture, and now you show up to fix my front door."

"It's no biggie," he said. "Also, I'm not a stranger. I'm actually your neighbor."

"What? Where do you live?"

"Half a mile down the road here," Ezra said, pointing south. "That's how I got this listing. I'd been driving past this place since I moved to Tarburton, and I was wondering who owned it. It's a gorgeous piece of property, as you've probably figured out by now. I looked up the tax records and contacted James Heywood and asked if he was interested in selling the place. He said people had been asking about buying it for years, but he wasn't quite ready to let it go. I just happened to be in the right place at the right time."

"Oh. Wait. So you're not originally from Tarburton?"

"Nope. I'm a newcomer, like you." He gave her a wink. "We newbies have to stick together, don't you think?"

Thirty minutes later she heard a rapping at the front door. Ezra handed her a set of keys. "Okay, that's done." He pointed to his toolbox. "If you want, I can take a look at that stopped-up sink you mentioned."

"You do plumbing?"

"Just the simple stuff."

She stood in the bathroom doorway and watched while he wiggled his upper torso beneath the bathroom vanity. "Can you get me that big monkey wrench? It's in the bottom of the toolbox."

Ivy handed him a wrench.

"That's a socket wrench."

She handed him the only other wrench-like object in the box.

Ezra grunted his approval. After some prolonged banging, and at least one muffled curse word, he extricated himself from the vanity cabinet with a curved piece of pipe in hand. "Here's your problem," he said. "Probably fifty years of built-up gunk."

"Ick," Ivy said. "Can it be fixed?"

"Sure. I'll just rinse it out in the bathtub. Word to the wise, get yourself some drain cleaner and run it through there on the regular."

"Awesome," Ivy said, shifting uncomfortably from foot to foot. "Look, neighbor or no neighbor, I can't let you do all these repairs for free."

"You're right," Ezra agreed. "You got any coffee?"

"It's just instant. My coffeemaker is on the moving truck."

He grimaced. "Better than nothing, I guess. That's my fee. A cup of hot coffee. I like mine with cream. And sugar. Is that a problem?"

She smiled despite herself. "I think I can handle that."

"Cool. I'll be done here in ten minutes."

Ivy hummed under her breath as she brewed the coffee and set out mugs and a plate. She unwrapped Mrs. Huddleston's cake and shuddered slightly. It was gooey and chocolatey with what looked like melted marshmallow topping. She placed a huge slice of cake on Ezra's plate and set it on the table.

"Man, that coffee smells instant," he announced as he walked into the kitchen.

"Sit." Ivy pointed at the single chair pulled up to the wooden table.

"But where'll you sit?" he asked.

"I'll just lean against the counter and look decorative," Ivy said.

"This doesn't feel right," he groused, easing onto the chair. "My mom would say she raised me better than this."

"My house, my rules," Ivy said lightly. She took a sip of coffee. "Thanks again for coming to my rescue. I'm afraid I haven't been a very gracious hostess."

Ezra looked down at the cake. "Don't tell me you baked this in your spare time." He shoved a forkful of it in his mouth, chewed, and grinned. "Oh my gawd," he drawled. "This stuff is incredible."

"Glad you like it," she said. "It was a gift from Sally Huddleston. Do you know her?"

He took another bite of cake and washed it down with a gulp of coffee. "Never met the lady. Is there a Mr. Huddleston? If not, I might have to propose."

"I don't actually know if she's single. But if you like mature women, Sally's your gal. I'm guessing she's in her fifties."

"That's cool," Ezra said. He pointed his fork at Ivy. "You're not having any cake?"

"I don't really enjoy sweets," Ivy said.

His eyes widened. "For real? Is it some kind of diet thing? I mean, not to get personal or anything, but seems to me you could stand to eat a few cheeseburgers."

"I just don't like sweets," Ivy said. "Never have."

"Not even as a kid? Like, no trick-or-treat candy? No pumpkin pie or birthday cake, or, I don't know, Easter basket PEEPS?" He scooped up another bite of cake. "PEEPS! I freakin' love Easter PEEPS."

"Maybe when I was really little." Ivy wanted to get off this topic. "So, earlier you said something about when you moved here? I somehow assumed you were a native."

Ezra took a last bite of cake and sat back from the table. "Nope. Born and raised in a little town in South Carolina. I moved here about a year ago."

"Why Tarburton, of all places?"

He looked down at his plate, chasing a gooey chocolate crumb around with the side of his fork. "Why does anyone move to a new place? I used to have family living in the area. I was working in banking in Charlotte. Trust me, there is nobody in Charlotte who does *not* work in banking. Like insurance in Hartford, or tech in California. I needed a change. Got my real estate license, and ended up here." He took a sip of coffee and pointed at her. "Your turn."

"Me? I got divorced. My ex and I owned the company together, and it was more than awkward, especially after I figured out his new squeeze was our biggest client."

Ezra winced. "Superawkward."

"Exactly. He bought out my share of the business, and our house. And then I had this bizarre urge to buy a broken-down farmhouse and fix it up. There's probably something Freudian there. I'll let you figure it out."

Ezra looked longingly at the remainder of the cake on the counter. Ivy laughed, cut off another slab, and added it to his plate.

He attacked the second slice of cake with enthusiasm.

"Something I've been wanting to ask you."

"Not about the Christmas lights, I hope."

"No. I'm just fascinated with the fact that you made an offer on this house, and bought it, without ever having seen it. Kind of a ballsy move."

"And totally unlike me," Ivy admitted. "The truth is, I'd been thinking about making a big change for months. I'd been browsing real estate listings, sort of daydreaming. But something came over me when I saw this place. It just . . . felt right. When you let me know there was another offer on the table, I think I came down with a bad case of FOMO."

Ezra nodded. "Feeding frenzy. It's a real thing. Tell me again what kind of work you do? Something creative, right?"

"Marketing and public relations."

"What kind of marketing?" he asked.

She sighed. "The lame kind, apparently. I seem to have lost my creative mojo. I got an email this morning from my biggest client — my only client, actually — and they're basically rejecting the campaign I've been working on for months and months."

"Ouch. Who's the client?"

"They're a big national home builder. I have to say, I'm not surprised. My heart's just not in it. They build these huge subdivisions with hundreds and hundreds of houses, all from the same cookie-cutter models."

"What can you do?" Ezra asked.

"I'm not sure. I've never had a client reject my work before. I was hoping moving here might be the spark to light my creative fire, but nothing seems to be working."

"Give it time," he advised. "You've been here what, three days?"

Punkin wandered into the kitchen and went immediately to Ezra, placing one muddy paw on their guest's lap. Ezra chuckled and obligingly scratched the setter's ears. "Good boy," he said.

"I can't believe he's doing that," Ivy said. "He's usually pretty standoffish with strangers."

"I keep telling you, I'm not a stranger," Ezra chided. He stood and placed his plate and coffee cup in the sink. "I took the liberty of measuring that broken windowpane in your room and the back bedroom. If you want, I can pick up some glass at the hardware store and replace the panes. How's tomorrow?"

"Tomorrow's good, but honestly, don't you have better things to do? Ezra, I appreciate it, but I don't know how I can repay your generosity."

"You could let me take you to dinner, for starters," he said. Then he pointed to the hunk of cake on the kitchen counter and grinned. "And I wouldn't say no to the rest of that cake, if you're not going to eat it."

Ivy felt herself blushing. "How about this?

You let me cook dinner for you. Not like a date. More as, like, a neighbor thing."

Ezra's grin faded momentarily. "Not really what I had in mind, but I guess it's a start."

Chapter 6

Ivy stood, shivering, staring at the thermostat. No heat. Temperatures had plummeted overnight. She'd burrowed deeper under the sleeping bag and quilt and finally, at daylight, she'd faced facts. No heat.

She bundled up in her warmest clothes, donned two pairs of socks and her boots, and went down to the basement to check out the furnace. It was cold and silent. How old was this thing? James Heywood had mentioned that his in-laws had only installed central heat in the eighties. Which meant her furnace was beyond middle-aged and facing obsolescence.

"Nooo!" she wailed, trudging back up the stairs. The chicks were peeping loudly from their cardboard crate.

She carried the crate into the chilly kitchen and set it on the table. "Hang in there, girls," she told them. "I'll have you warmed up in a second." She turned on the oven and opened the door. Nothing. No blue flame. Nada.

It occurred to her that both the furnace and her stove were gas fueled. That was the good news. The bad news was that her propane tank was probably empty.

The chickens were still chirping their complaints about the cold. She dashed into the bedroom and brought back the quilt, which she draped over the box, being careful not to cover the ventilation holes.

She picked up her phone to call Ezra Wheeler to ask about having the propane tank refilled. Which was when she noticed she'd missed a call during her basement expedition.

The caller, Acme Movers, who should have been pulling into her driveway right about now with her furniture, had left a voicemail:

"Uh, hi. This is Jenny from Acme Movers Dispatch. Just wanted to let you know we've had a little mix-up down here in Atlanta. Seems like your load got sent down to Fort Myers. Your new delivery date is Wednesday. You can call our office if you have any questions. Sorry about that!"

Ivy buried her face in her hands. She was cold and hungry and pissed. She needed caffeine. She trudged into the bathroom, turned on the taps, got undressed, and stepped into the shower.

She was sure her shriek could be heard all over the county. Apparently, her hot-water heater was also propane fueled. She dressed with lightning speed.

Her call to Ezra Wheeler went directly to voicemail. She was having that kind of morning.

Punkin met her at the door with his leash in his mouth. "Okay, boy, we'll warm up walking into town."

"Stay here and be good, and I'll bring you a treat," Ivy said as she tethered Punkin loosely to the bike rack outside the café.

The Coffee Cup had hot coffee, grits, biscuits, bacon, and eggs and Ivy ordered it all. No sign today of the ponytailed waitress she'd encountered the previous day. She was sitting at a table by a sun-soaked window, clutching her coffee mug in both hands, when her new friend Phoebe walked in.

Ivy waved her over to her table and Phoebe sat down.

"What brings you to town so early? I thought you said your movers were coming this morning?"

"I thought so too," Ivy said, her expression grim. "No movers. No heat, no hot water. Seems like my propane tank is empty."

"Ohhhh," Phoebe said. "You poor thing."

The waitress appeared. "Hi, Phoebe, whatcha having?"

"Just coffee, Angela. Black, please."

"No biscuits? Or doughnuts?"

"Just the coffee," Phoebe said firmly.

When their server was gone, Phoebe leaned in to whisper, "Everybody in here is lookin' at you."

"Yeah, I kind of noticed that," Ivy said. "Must be a slow news day."

"Every day is a slow news day in Tarburton. You're kind of the talk of the town. Folks are wondering why a gorgeous city girl like you wanted to buy a falling-down farmhouse in a hick town like this way off in the mountains."

Ivy laughed. "Days like today, I wonder that myself. But I can assure you, it's nothing sinister. It's peaceful here. No crime, no traffic like Atlanta. No . . . memories."

Phoebe motioned toward Ivy's ringless hands, especially the left, which bore a pale, untanned band of skin on the ring finger.

"He hurt you bad, huh?"

"Let's just say we hurt each other. And since I can work anywhere I want, I chose here."

"Here?" Phoebe looked around the homely diner. "There's not but three stoplights — and one, the one in front of First Baptist, is really only a blinking light. No mall, no clubs, no fun."

"And why are you here?" Ivy asked.

"Born and raised here. Like my mama and daddy." Phoebe leaned in and lowered her voice. "I'll tell you a secret. I'm not fixing on staying here much longer. My boyfriend, Cody, is deployed. He's an Army Ranger. And where he's at is so supersecret he can't even tell me where it is. But he'll be home in two weeks, and then . . ."

She looked around the café to make sure nobody could overhear. "You can't tell a soul this next part, okay?"

"That's easy. I don't know a soul in Tarburton."

"You know me. And you know that cute Ezra Wheeler."

"How do you know . . ." Ivy's voice trailed off. "Oh yeah. Small town. Anyway, your secret is safe with me."

Phoebe took a deep breath. "We're gonna elope. We've got it all planned out. It'll be so romantic. He'll be home two days before Christmas. Mr. Schoonover, he's the city clerk you met, he'll give us our marriage license, and Judge Briggs, I've known him since forever, I think he'd marry us, but just in case, I think we'll go over to the next county and find a justice of the peace. And then we honeymoon in Gatlinburg."

"That does sound romantic," Ivy said, thinking about her own lavish wedding, with eight bridesmaids and as many groomsmen, and the flurry of parties and celebrations. And then, six years later, she was single again.

"Does your family know about your wedding plans?" Ivy asked.

Phoebe looked away and a faint red flush crept into her cheeks. "No. Cody's kind of my secret."

"Why is that?"

"Well . . ." Phoebe fiddled with the fringe of her scarf. "They've never met him. So they'd never approve."

"Oh." Ivy wondered if she should pry into her new friend's personal life.

"How did you meet him?"

The younger woman perked back up again. "Online! He friended me, and liked a bunch of my pictures, and we started talking and he just . . . gets me. You know? He's not like any of the guys around here. All they care about is ball games and fishing and hunting. But Cody, he cares about big, important stuff. And he's serving our country!" She smiled shyly. "You want to see his picture?"

"Of course!"

Phoebe took out her phone and began scrolling through her camera roll. She thrust the phone at Ivy. "Isn't he cute?"

Ivy studied the photos. Cody the Ranger was, indeed, cute. The photos showed a muscular twentysomething, grinning into the camera, looking like an Army recruitment poster in his fatigues, or standing, bare chested, flexing his six-pack abs and considerable biceps. There were photos of Cody in his dress uniform, with a chest full of medals, and pictures of Cody cutting up in a bar with beers and buddies.

The thing that struck Ivy was that Cody looked too good to be true.

"So you two have never met in real life? Not even on FaceTime or Skype?"

"He can't do that kind of stuff, because he's in a high-security location with sketchy Wi-Fi and they have strict regulations about FaceTime kinds of stuff. But we email and text and talk on a secure phone as often as we can."

"How long have you two known each other?" Ivy asked.

"In real time, about eight months. My mama and daddy only knew each other for three months before they got married and they were married twenty-five years!"

"Oh. . . ." Ivy let the word hang there and Phoebe immediately picked up on her reaction.

"I can tell you don't approve. You probably think Cody's one of those online scammers, right?"

"It did occur to me," Ivy admitted.

Phoebe loosened the scarf around her neck and pulled a thin gold chain from beneath the collar of her blouse. A heavy gold signet ring hung from it. Phoebe kissed the ring, then tucked it back under her neckline.

"That's Cody's class ring," she said proudly. "Trolls don't send rings to girls. And they don't send flowers every month on the tenth, because that's our date-a-versary."

"No, they probably don't," Ivy said. "He sends you flowers? So nice!"

"Daisies. Because he knows they're my favorite. I mentioned it when we first started dating and he remembered. He remembers everything."

"Cody sounds like a sweet, thoughtful man," Ivy said.

"He's awesome," Phoebe agreed, beaming. She glanced at the phone she was still holding in her hand. "Oops! I'd better get back to work. But I meant to ask, how is it going with your search for Carlette and Everett?"

"I've been so busy with the house, I haven't really had time to do more research," Ivy said. "But I did find a whole trunk full of Santa Bob's old letters and files, so I'm going to look through all that stuff to see if I can find any clues."

"Let me know if you discover anything," Phoebe said. "Mom would love to find out what happened to her old friend."

"I just had a thought," Ivy said. "Can you call her and ask what her address was when she lived across the street from Carlette's family?"

"I don't have to ask her; I know it by heart. Seven-oh-two Spruce Street. Mom used to ride me past her childhood home all the time and point it out. I don't think anyone has lived there in a long time, though. Why do you ask?"

"Your mother said someone in Carlette's family owned the house they were living in while her daddy was overseas. Who knows? Maybe whoever lives there now will know something."

Phoebe shook her head. "You're really into this, aren't you?"

"I guess I am," Ivy said lightly. "Besides, what else have I got to do? My furniture is stuck down in Florida somewhere, and I'm up here with no heat and no hot water. And no business."

CHAPTER 7

Ivy and Punkin walked past the Main Street storefronts, where shopkeepers were just opening their doors for the day. All the streets around the downtown area were named for trees: Oak, Maple, Magnolia, Cedar . . .

She checked her phone for a map of Tarburton and discovered that Spruce Street was only three blocks east of where she was currently standing.

Ten minutes later, she was standing in front of 702 Spruce. The little white cottage with green-and-white-striped awnings must have been a showplace at one time. But now pickets were missing from the white fence that surrounded the lot. The overgrown foundation plantings towered over the roofline. And the awnings themselves were so ragged and sagging it looked like the house was frowning.

The house directly across the street, 705,

was a tidy redbrick ranch. White-painted rocks interspersed with miniature American flags surrounded neatly trimmed beds of shrubbery. An aging Chevy was parked in the driveway and there was a wreath with a jaunty red, white, and blue–striped bow hanging on the front door.

Punkin sat obediently on the front stoop while Ivy rang the doorbell. Nothing. She waited a full minute and then rang again. Punkin looked up expectantly.

"One more time?" she asked.

The dog's tail wagged agreement. "If you insist," Ivy said. Her finger was poised over the bell when a man's voice called out from inside, "Hold your horses! I'm coming!"

Finally, the door opened a few inches. The security chain was engaged, and a pair of pale blue eyes glared at her from behind thick-lensed wire-rimmed glasses.

"Whatever you're selling, we don't want any," the man said.

"I'm not selling anything," Ivy said. "I'm sorry for disturbing you but —"

"Name?" the man demanded.

"Huh?" Ivy was taken aback. "Uh, I'm Ivy Perkins, and this is my dog, Punkin."

"Punkin Perkins?" The old man's thin lips cracked a smile. "That's a good one. I love a good alliteration. What do you want with me, Ivy Perkins?"

"Just some information." Ivy hadn't really planned her line of questioning because she hadn't really expected anyone to answer the door.

"Is this a poll? Because I don't discuss my politics or my religion. Not with anybody." He started to close the door.

"No, sir," Ivy said quickly. "I'm looking for information about a family that lived here a really long time ago. I think it would have been during the late nineteen-sixties or early seventies."

The old man's expression softened. He slid the chain aside and opened the door. "Maybe you'd better come inside and explain yourself, Miss Perkins."

Her host leaned on his walker and lowered himself into a leather recliner. He motioned to the sofa. "Sit there. Is Punkin house-trained? I don't want my carpet ruined."

"Yes, sir," Ivy said, seating herself on the sofa with Punkin crouched at her feet. "He's very well trained." The house was neat as a pin and as hot as an oven. Any oven except for the one at Ivy's house. A small ceramic Christmas tree stood on a table in the corner of the room.

"By the way, I'm Lawrence E. Jones. I've

owned this house since 1961. Now what's this all about?"

"Jones?" Ivy sat up straight on the sofa. "Then, are you related to Diana Jones? And her daughter, Carlette?"

Mr. Jones clutched the handles of his walker. "Diana was my daughter-in-law. And Carlette was my granddaughter."

Ivy realized she was holding her breath. She exhaled slowly. "And Everett?"

"Was my son." He removed his glasses and wiped them on the sleeve of his sweater. Or the top layer of sweater. From where Ivy sat, it appeared that her host was wearing at least three sweaters. The outermost sweater was a navy blue cardigan, pilled on the front and unraveling at the sleeve.

"Why are you asking about my son and his family?"

"It's a long story," Ivy began. "I'm new in Tarburton. I just bought a farmhouse about a mile out of town. Maybe you knew Bob and Betty Rae Rose?"

"You bought Four Roses Farm?"

"Yes. I just moved in last week."

"Does your husband farm?"

"No. I'm divorced."

"So you're the farmer?" He looked skeptical.

"Well, not yet. I mean, I have some chickens. And I have plans for a big garden, in the spring. I've already ordered my seeds."

"What's a young woman like you want with a decrepit old farmhouse like that? Nobody's lived out there for years and years."

"It's not decrepit." Ivy was offended on behalf of her new home. "It's . . . well loved. It needs some work, that's all. The roof is sound, and the plumbing works. . . ."

"I see." Mr. Jones looked unconvinced.

"The thing is, the house came furnished, and I was cleaning out a closet in the master bedroom, and I found an old Santa Claus suit."

"Santa Bob," Mr. Jones said, nodding. "He was pretty much a legend in these parts. Betty Rae too. They were quite a couple. The wife and I used to take our little boy to see them at Atkins Department Store. And then we'd ride out to their place to see all the Christmas lights."

"And Everett was that little boy?"

"That's right." His blue eyes searched her face. "Are you going to tell me what this has to do with my son?"

Ivy took the note from her pocket and handed it to Lawrence E. Jones. "I found this in the pocket of the Santa suit. It . . . touched me. I was intrigued."

The old man read the note, tracing the childish scrawl with a bony fingertip. "Oh my." He folded the note and handed it back. "Oh my." He found a neatly pressed handkerchief in the pocket of his sweater and dabbed at his eyes. "Oh my goodness."

Punkin crept closer to Mr. Jones's chair. Ivy was astonished as the dog gently laid his muzzle in the old man's lap.

"I take it . . . Carlette didn't get her Christmas wish?" she asked.

"No," Mr. Jones said softly. "Everett was a helicopter pilot with the Eighty-second Airborne. His chopper was shot down and he was declared missing in action in September of 1971. Diana didn't want to tell Carlette what had happened, because, well, we were all praying he'd somehow be found alive."

"I see." Ivy folded and unfolded her hands in her lap, feeling her own eyes filling with unexpected tears.

"The Army didn't officially declare him dead until three years later when the remains of the helicopter and Ev and the rest of his crew were found way out in the jungle," Mr. Jones went on. "The waiting to hear was awful. For all of us, but most of all, for Diana. She and my granddaughter were living here in this house, because my company transferred me out to Seattle. She decided to stay here in Tarburton while Ev was overseas, because it was a free place to live."

Ivy looked puzzled.

"Anyway, after we finally got the news that Everett was missing, Diana decided to move closer to her own folks, who lived down in South Carolina."

"That makes sense," Ivy said. "I talked to a neighbor, Sally Huddleston, who told me she and Carlette were best friends, but she lost track of Carlette, after the family moved away."

He looked up sharply. "Sally? That must be the same little girl who lived across the street — in that house with the awnings. You talked to her?"

"Yes. I've become friends with her daughter Phoebe, who works at the courthouse."

"Could I see the note again?" He held out his hand and she gave him the note.

He studied it closely.

"What about Carlette?" Ivy persisted. "And her mom? Where are they now?"

Lawrence Jones looked up. "I don't mean to be rude, but why do you want to know? They're strangers to you, right?"

"It's the note," Ivy said slowly. "It's like a clue. Isn't it? A little mystery. And since I found the note, somehow it feels like my responsibility. I've been wondering, since I found it, about Carlette, and her mama. And, of course, Everett. I've been wondering about Santa Bob too. I found a trunk full of letters from children to him, old Santa photos, and newspaper clippings. But why did he keep this one note, in the pocket of that suit? What was special about that particular letter?"

"I can't answer that," Mr. Jones said sadly. "If you find Carlette, maybe you could ask her yourself."

Slowly, he pulled himself up from the chair and, with the aid of the walker, left the room. When he returned, he was holding a large, hinged picture frame, which he handed to Ivy.

The photo on the left showed a handsome young soldier in uniform, standing proudly in front of an American flag. "That's Ev," Mr. Jones said, pointing. The photo on the right showed a young teenage girl, with long coppery hair, braces, and a wisp of a smile.

"And that's Carlette. Her eighth-grade school picture. It's the last photo I have of her."

Ivy handed the photo frame back to her host. "What happened?"

He lowered himself into his armchair,

grimacing from the effort, and Punkin sat expectantly at his feet.

"The first couple years after she and her mom moved away, we'd hear from Diana pretty regular. We were still living out in Seattle, but we'd visit when we could, at Christmas and such. But then Polly, my wife, got sick with heart disease, and we couldn't travel as much. She died in 1976. When Diana didn't come to the funeral, didn't even send a card, well, that hurt. I figured something was going on, but I kept on writing, sending birthday cards and such to Carlette."

"Did Carlette write back, or call?"

Mr. Jones turned the frame over and slid the cardboard backing away from the girl's photo. A color postcard and a thick square of vellum slid out. His hand shook as he handed both to his guest.

The front of the postcard featured a color photo of Cinderella Castle at Disney World. The girlish handwriting on the back was full of flourishes:

Hi, Granddaddy. We are at Disney World, having a great time. Mom said I shouldn't tell you, but I think you should know that she got married, and we are here on her honeymoon. Walter says he was Daddy's friend in the Army. I miss you and I'm sorry about Granny. Love, Carlette.

Ivy raised an eyebrow.

"Walter Ramsberger was best man at Ev and Diana's wedding. He and Ev went through basic training together and shipped out to Vietnam at the same time. Walter came back, but like I said, Ev didn't."

The other card was a formal graduation announcement:

MR. AND MRS. WALTER RAMSBERGER ANNOUNCE THE GRADUATION OF THEIR DAUGHTER, CARLETTE DIANE, FROM ROCKY SHOALS SENIOR HIGH SCHOOL, FORT MILL, S.C., MAY 5, 1982.

"I sent her a graduation card with a hundred-dollar bill in it," the old man said. "Mailed to the last address I had for Diana. But I guess they must have moved, because the card came back unopened."

His hand strayed to Punkin's head, and he stroked the dog's ears.

"So you completely lost touch with your granddaughter?" Ivy said. "That's so sad."

"It is," he agreed. "I moved back here to this house, after Polly died. I brought my sweetheart home to be buried in the family plot at Piney Grove, like she wanted. Everett's remains are there too. I had no ties to Seattle, and well, I keep hoping, someday, I'll hear that doorbell ring and I'll look out and see that little girl standing on my doorstep again."

He busied himself putting the two cards back into the picture frame, and when he looked up again tears glistened behind the glasses. "Maybe that's why I answered the door today. I'm a foolish old man, I know. Carlette would be a grown woman now. Might have grandkids of her own. I wonder if I'd recognize her, if I saw her again. Wouldn't that be something?"

"Have you ever tried to track her down?" Ivy asked, her voice gentle.

"I wouldn't know where to start," Mr. Jones said. "Anyway, what's the point? All that is ancient history now." His hands shook badly as he stroked Punkin's head, and Ivy felt guilty for knocking on this stranger's door and stirring up old heartache.

"Okay," she said, nodding agreement. "I understand." She hesitated. "Would you like to keep Carlette's note?"

Mr. Jones seemed surprised by her offer. "Yes," he said finally. "I think I would." He pulled himself up from his armchair and hobbled over to the television, an old-fashioned console affair with a bulbous screen and rabbit-ear antennas. He plucked a cut-glass jar from the top of the console.

He opened the jar and held it out to Ivy. "Here. Take one."

The jar was full of cellophane-wrapped chocolate candies. Ivy took one and gave him a questioning look.

"These were Carlette's favorites. I always keep them in the house. Don't eat a lot of sweets myself, except for these."

"I'm not really a sweets person either," Ivy confessed.

"Try one of these," Mr. Jones urged. "I buy 'em from a shop here in town. They're different. Not too sweet. More minty."

She obligingly peeled the wrapper away and tasted. He was right. The candy was dark chocolate, sweet with just a hint of pepper and a big dose of mint.

"Pretty good," she admitted.

Lawrence Jones helped himself to a piece of candy. "I guess I just like the taste of peppermint. It reminds me of Christmas. And hope."

Chapter 8

Ivy read and reread the email from her home-builder client. The words "severing our relationship" swam before her eyes. A nice way of saying she was fired.

It shouldn't have come as a surprise, but it had. She'd never been fired before, never really failed at anything. Well, except at marriage. So now she was oh for two in just the past nine months.

She picked up a piece of the chocolate candy Lawrence Jones had pressed upon her, peeled off the cellophane, and sucked. The smell of peppermint and the slight peppery tang of the candy somehow eased the sting of rejection. She examined the printing on the wrapper and typed the company's name into her computer's search engine.

"Oh no," she muttered, looking down at the company website. It looked like it had been designed by someone with less than a passing understanding of graphic design.

Or public relations, or marketing.

It was clunky, even ugly. But she did manage to learn that Langley Sweets had been around for ninety years, was still owned by a member of the Langley family, Nancy Langley Bergstrom, and that their best-known product was the one she was holding in her hand — Dark Chocolate Peppery-Mint Patties.

"Not a bad name," Ivy mused, but it, and the product itself, was the only thing to like about the public face of Langley Sweets. The website didn't even have a link to buy the product, for heaven's sake. The packaging, company logo, all of it, was completely mediocre and utterly charmless. There was a photo of the candy shop on the website, and she realized she'd passed the business several times on her trips downtown, without ever taking notice of it.

Ivy took another tentative taste of the PepperyMint. She closed her eyes and inhaled. Lawrence Jones was right. These candies were special. They conjured up hope, and holidays, and, well, even a little bit of magic.

She opened her laptop and began typing, her fingers flying across the keyboard as she conjured up a new advertising campaign for PepperyMint Patties.

"PepperyMint: So good they'll take your

breath away!"

But it wasn't just words this brand needed; they needed new images too. Ivy's mind turned to the old Christmas cards and Santa Claus photos and letters she'd discovered in the trunk currently residing in the otherwise-empty guest bedroom.

Ivy sat cross-legged on the floor of the bedroom. The folders of cards, letters, and photos were spilled haphazardly across the top layer of items in the trunk.

The letters to Santa tugged at her heartstrings.

Dear Santa: Please bring me an Easy-Bake Oven so I can help my mama cook. Her oven don't work. Your friend, Amanda.

Santa Bob had made some kind of chicken-scratch notes on the back of the letter. Ivy could make out what looked like an address, but the rest was illegible.

Dear Santa: I would like a real big-leaguer catcher's glove for Christmas. My dad says his old glove is good enough, but it's way too big. P.S. We are moving soon, because my dad needs to find a job, but

Mama says you'll know where to find us.
Sinserly, Mack Purdom.

Stapled to the bottom of the letter was what looked like a yellowing page torn from an old Sears, Roebuck catalog with a catcher's mitt circled in red.

There were dozens of other letters, with requests for dolls, bicycles, skateboards, and even one for a real live panda bear, but only a few had notes scribbled on them — presumably by Santa himself. Ivy wondered idly about the meaning of the scribbles.

The old greeting cards were a treasure trove of ideas, with their retro images of impish elves, dancing Christmas trees, and grinning snowmen.

One card in particular caught her interest. The illustration depicted two red-garbed pixies playing tug-of-war with a candy cane.

"Perfect," Ivy said, setting the card aside. She dug farther into the trunk, marveling that each layer seemed to reveal another ring representing the life of the former owners of Four Roses Farm.

The department store Santa pictures were treasures in themselves, each showing Santa Bob, photographed through the ages, always beaming at a child. Sometimes the children looked in awe at Santa, other children were laughing, and still others were captured with tear-stained, screaming faces. On the back of each photo was taped a slip of paper with a serial number, and the child's name, neatly typed.

As she shuffled through the photographs, she came to one that stopped her cold. A little girl was seated on Santa Bob's lap, tugging solemnly at his beard. Ivy turned the photo over and her breath caught in her throat. "Carlette Jones."

Ivy studied the photo more closely. Carlette had a large candy cane clutched in her left hand. She was dressed in a red plaid dress with a starched crinoline, white tights, and black patent-leather Mary Janes. Ivy too had once worn similar shoes, which crackled when she walked and pinched her toes.

And was it her imagination? Or did Santa seem to be listening more intently to this child's fondest wish?

She set Carlette's photo on top of the file of photographs and decided she would deliver it to Lawrence Jones. And maybe, she thought, the Langley candy company would be interested in displaying these relics of bygone days in their dusty little shop.

Beneath the letters, cards, and photographs in the trunk, Ivy found a large cardboard box. She lifted it out and brushed the dust from the top. Opening it, she found a glittering wonderland of vintage Shiny Brite glass Christmas tree ornaments, each resting in a nest of crumpled tissue paper.

Ivy removed each ornament from the box and marveled over the jewel-like colors, some dusted with glass glitter, others indented, or hand-painted. She stopped counting at fifty.

Ivy peered down into the trunk, which seemed to her to be more treasure chest than footlocker. On the very bottom of the trunk she found another cardboard box, this one full of Christmas tree lights. But these were not ordinary lights; they were red, green, and yellow bubble lights.

Her nana had lights like these on her Christmas tree. Ivy could remember sitting beneath the tree, looking up at the bubbling fluid in the candle-shaped bulbs with a sense of childlike wonder.

Punkin wandered into the room and sniffed the contents of the box, wagging his tail as if in approval.

"I agree, Punkin. These are too magical to hide away again," Ivy said. She stood and dusted her hands on the seat of her jeans, then began carrying the boxes of lights and ornaments into the living room.

She held her breath as she plugged in the first string of bubble lights, praying she wouldn't start an electrical fire in her new home. But the lights blinked on and immediately began to glow.

"Okay," she said, looking down at the setter. "You're right. Just because we don't have a tree, or any furniture, come to think of it, that doesn't mean we can't have lights."

She swagged the lights across the fireplace mantel, then stepped back to admire the effect. Yup. Magical.

In a kitchen cupboard, she found a large green Pyrex mixing bowl. Carrying it into the living room, she heaped a dozen of the showiest ornaments into the bowl and set it on the mantel. She scattered the rest of the ornaments across the top of the mantel and smiled ruefully. Christmas hadn't just arrived at Four Roses Farm. It had been here all along, waiting for her to discover it.

In the morning, she dressed for success for the first time since arriving in Tarburton: a silk blouse, woolen slacks, and her favorite tweed blazer. She packed her briefcase with her laptop, an assortment of the Santa photos and letters, and the vintage greeting cards, including the one that had inspired the previous night's burst of creativity.

Punkin followed her to the front door, wagging his tail, anticipating a romp in the woods or a walk to town. She leaned down and scratched his ears. "Sorry, pal. I've got work to do."

He wagged his tail harder and licked her hand. "All right," she relented. "But you can't go inside the candy store. No dogs allowed!"

Bells jingled as she pushed through the door into Langley Sweets. A middle-aged woman dressed in a red-and-white-striped apron stood behind the candy counter waiting on two elderly customers who were taste-testing different varieties of fudge.

"Welcome!" the clerk said, looking up. "We're just testing a new batch of fudge. Want to try a piece?" She held out a fluted paper cup holding a square of fudge dotted with shards of peppermint candy.

"Oh, uh, well . . ."

"Go ahead," one of the other customers urged. "It's delicious. Everything Nancy makes is wonderful. I'm taking a pound to my bridge club luncheon."

Ivy gulped and decided to take one for the team. She popped the fudge in her mouth and was surprised by the sensations assaulting her taste buds. Sweet, yes, but with peppery undernotes and something . . . ineffable.

"It's delicious," Ivy blurted out. "And I don't like candy."

The clerk laughed. "Oh my. I've never met anyone who didn't like candy."

One of the old ladies nudged the other. "Imagine that!"

The two women paid for their purchases, gave Ivy a long, puzzled look, then exited the candy shop.

"Now, how can I help you?" the clerk asked, her eyes crinkling with barely suppressed mirth. "I take it you must be here to buy a gift for someone who *does* like sweets?"

Ivy took a deep breath. "Actually, I'm looking for Nancy Langley Bergstrom. Is she around today?"

"I'm Nancy," the clerk said. "President, CEO, and chief candymaker. Also, bottle washer, janitor, and head of the shipping department."

"Okay. Hi, Nancy. I'm Ivy Perkins, and I have a business proposition for you."

The candymaker's smile faded. "I'm sorry. If you're selling something, well, I'm not really in a position to buy anything at this time." She leaned across the counter and looked straight into Ivy's eyes. "In fact, I'm afraid we'll be closing the store right after Christmas."

"Oh no!" Ivy exclaimed. "How sad."

"You don't even know," Nancy Bergstrom agreed. "I've tried everything. New flavors, sale pricing, online offers. But I'm just out of ideas. And energy. This company has been in my family for ninety years. And I'm the one who will be the one to turn off the lights and lock the door and walk away. I feel like such a failure."

"But you're not a failure," Ivy protested. "Not at candy. As I said, I don't eat sweets, but your Dark Chocolate PepperyMint Patties — they're like nothing I've ever tasted before. In fact, that's why I came here today. I wanted to talk to you about your marketing. Your packaging, your online presence — forgive me, but they don't reflect your product. At all."

"And you're an expert at those kinds of things?" Nancy asked, one eyebrow raised.

"Actually, I am," Ivy said. "I have my own marketing and public relations firm. Like you, I'm a small, one-woman shop. And I really believe I can help you."

"Thanks," Nancy said, "but I really don't think —"

They heard a scratching at the front window. Ivy looked over to see Punkin, standing on his back legs, scratching at the display window.

"Is that your dog?" Nancy Bergstrom asked.

"Yes. Sorry. He's gotten sort of . . . clingy since I moved here. Maybe I'd better put him in the car."

"He's adorable," Nancy said. "It's too cold for him to be outside. Let's bring him in. He can hang out in the back room with my dog. Sugar is old and mostly blind, so she won't mind."

"There," Nancy said, after the two dogs were companionably curled beneath a table in the back room. "Now, tell me again what it is you're trying to sell that I can't afford?"

Ivy set her laptop on the table and opened the file with the ad campaign she'd designed for Langley Sweets, featuring retro elves, beaming Santas, and wide-eyed children.

"Now, this would just be your seasonal holiday campaign," Ivy explained. "We'd do other graphics for the rest of the year, but the feel would be the same — retro, fun, sweet. And the slogan would be used year-round."

Nancy shook her head and bit her lip. "I love it. Truly. But I can't afford anything like this. And anyway, it's really too late —"

"You don't understand. There's no charge.

It's free."

Nancy stared. "An advertising campaign like this probably costs thousands of dollars. You don't even know me. Why would you do this for a stranger?"

Ivy repeated the words Ezra Wheeler had used when she tried to pay him for his handyman services. "I'm not a stranger. I'm actually your neighbor."

"You live here?"

"I just moved into the Four Roses farmhouse," Ivy said. "A new friend — do you know Lawrence Jones? — gave me some of your candy, and it was so different, so delicious, I looked up your website."

"I know Mr. Jones. Such a lovely man. And you're the new owner of Santa Bob's house? I didn't know it had sold. But welcome to Tarburton."

"About the website?" Ivy prompted.

"Oh that." Nancy grimaced. "I designed it myself. Pretty sad, huh?"

"Well, yeah, to tell you the truth, it's abysmal," Ivy said. "It doesn't reflect your product at all. Candy should be fun, right? Whimsical. And your candy is unique. I've never tasted anything like it."

"My great-grandfather's recipe," Nancy said modestly. "He made his own extracts and flavorings. I still use his original recipes."

"See," Ivy said excitedly. "That's what makes your product so unique. You should have that in your advertising."

"I guess," Nancy said. "But if I'm closing anyway . . ."

"Oh. Right. Exactly why are you closing? Did your rent go up?"

"No. I own the building outright. It's just . . . I'm single now; my son is grown and gone. It all feels so overwhelming."

"I get it," Ivy agreed. "I'm newly single myself."

She dug into her briefcase and brought out the vintage greeting cards and Santa photos and letters.

"Look," she said, fanning them out across the tabletop. "Aren't these great?"

"That's Santa Bob!" Nancy Bergstrom exclaimed, tapping one of the old photos. "And oh my gosh, that's Denise Gordon. We were in grade school together. I'd recognize that gap-toothed smile anywhere." She leafed through more photos. "I'd swear that's Kenny Zeigler. And this is his sister, Mary-Anne." She looked up at Ivy. "Where did you find these?"

"In a trunk at the house," Ivy said. "Santa Bob's son-in-law left them behind. He said he's not the sentimental type."

"Aww," Nancy said. "What are you going to do with them?"

"I thought maybe you'd like to use them in here in the store," Ivy said. "After the holidays, I'll see if the local historical society would like them. And all these Santa letters and old greeting cards — would you like to borrow them?"

Nancy was smiling down at the retro images. "I could make a darling window display. Folks could see if they recognize themselves, or family members. Maybe it would drum up more business."

"That's what I was thinking," Ivy agreed. "So, what do you say? Are you ready for a rebranding? And a new website? Think of it as a makeover for Langley Sweets?"

Nancy Bergstrom hesitated, then shrugged. "Sure. Why not? What have I got to lose? When do we start?"

"Right now," Ivy said. "I can get the website up today. I really think online orders — especially after Christmas is over — could revive your business." She filled the candymaker in on her plans, got the password for her social media accounts, and even, reluctantly, agreed to an initial payment — of PepperyMint Patties — for her services.

She leaned under the table and roused her sleeping dog. "Come on, Punkin. We've got one more stop to make."

Chapter 9

Lawrence Jones gazed down at the photo of his granddaughter and smiled wistfully. "This is how I remember Carlette. Always so serious. And always asking questions. Ev was like that too." He tapped the photo with his fingertip. "I remember this dress. My wife made it. She was so happy to have a little girl to sew dresses for."

"It's beautiful," Ivy said. "She was an adorable little girl."

"She looked a lot like my wife. Everyone said so."

Ivy looked around the tidy little living room. Her host had propped some Christmas cards on the mantel, beside a wooden manger scene, and there were two small wrapped packages under a tabletop Christmas tree that hadn't been there during her previous visit.

"A real Christmas tree?" she asked.

"Oh yes," her host said, nodding vigorously. "No fake trees for me. Nosirreebob! Nothing else smells as good as a fresh-cut Christmas tree. One of my neighbors always brings mine over and puts it up for me. Have you gotten your tree yet?"

"Don't think I'll bother with a tree this year," Ivy said. "I'm still in the middle of getting settled in at the farmhouse, and after all, it's just me."

"So what?" he said gently. "I'm the only one who'll see my tree, but it still makes me happy. I sit here and look at my tree all lit up, every night, and I remember the meaning of the tree and the Christmas season. My family might be mostly gone, but I still have my memories of them."

"It looks like you've already had a visit from Santa," Ivy observed, trying to change the subject.

"My great-nephew in Florida," Mr. Jones said. "His wife is very thoughtful. And she's quite the knitter." To demonstrate, he wiggled his toes in their bright orange knit booties with blue and orange tassels. "These are from last year. I have two more pairs in my closet, and some scarves and an afghan and some potholders and a toilet paper cover. And a hot-water bottle cover too."

"You'll never be cold," Ivy said, laughing. She stood up to leave, but Punkin stayed crouched beside the old man's chair.

"Come, Punkin!" she called. The dog wagged his tail but stayed put.

"It's the oddest thing," Ivy said. "Punkin was always standoffish with strangers. Maybe because he was a rescue. He was never mean, or aggressive, but he's always been sort of wary, if you know what I mean. But since we moved here, he seems to have lost some of his inhibitions. He's the same way with you as my real estate agent. It's like you're his instant best friends."

Mr. Jones scratched Punkin's ears. "You're never too old to have a new friend," he said.

She spotted Phoebe sitting alone in a booth in the corner of the diner. The clerk looked up and waved her over.

"Join me for lunch?" the girl asked.

"Love to. I gotta admit, eating alone is my least favorite part of being single," Ivy said.

"Mine too," Phoebe said.

Ivy eyed the girl's meal — black coffee, a hard-boiled egg, and three bedraggled leaves of lettuce.

"That's all you're having?" she asked.

The waitress arrived at their booth and Ivy ordered the day's special — chicken and dumplings and green beans.

Phoebe sighed enviously. "Maybe I'll just

inhale when your lunch arrives."

"I take it you're dieting?" Ivy asked. "Pretty hard to do during the holidays."

"It's the worst," Phoebe agreed. "But I've just got to lose ten more pounds before . . . you know."

"Oh, right," Ivy whispered. "Before you and Cody elope."

Ivy studied her friend from across the table. "Your hair is different too. You've gone blond, haven't you?"

The girl tucked a strand of hair behind her ear. "It's called Bombshell. You don't think it's too blond, right? My mom hates it."

"I think you're pretty just the way you are," Ivy said. "And Cody must think so too, or he wouldn't have asked you to marry him. Right?"

Phoebe stared down at her plate and her face colored slightly. "Well, the thing is . . ."

Ivy waited.

The waitress arrived at the table with Ivy's plate of food. The chicken and dumplings were steaming and sprinkled with bits of parsley, and the green beans were flecked with chunks of bacon.

"Oh Gawwwwd," Phoebe said, inhaling deeply. "That looks amazing."

"It's way more than I can eat," Ivy said,

shoving her plate toward Phoebe. "Don't you want to share?"

"Noooo," Phoebe said. "Don't tempt me." She sipped her black coffee. "Let's not talk about food. How are things coming at Four Roses Farm? Have you made any progress finding Carlette?"

"I didn't find Carlette, but I did find an old photo of her, sitting on Santa's lap," Ivy said.

She filled Phoebe in on the cache she'd discovered in Santa Bob's old trunk.

"I wonder if there's an old photo of me in there?" Phoebe said. "Mama and Daddy always took me to Atkins to see Santa when I was little."

"Could be," Ivy said. "Looking at all those vintage images, I got inspired. And I might have gotten myself a new client." She took a bite of the chicken and dumplings.

"Mmmm," she said. "Worth every calorie."

"Don't!" Phoebe begged. "Tell me about the new client."

"Have you ever had any PepperyMints from Langley Sweets?" Ivy asked.

"Sure. My grandmother loves their Cinnamon Twists. And I *used* to love their peppermint fudge."

"Right. Anyway, the first time I visited

Lawrence Jones, he gave me a piece of their dark chocolate peppermint candies. You know I don't eat sweets, right? But he insisted I taste one — and I was amazed. They're really so unique. Not like anything I've ever tasted before. I looked up the company on the internet, and their branding was just so pathetic — stale and utterly charmless. I sort of fell down the rabbit hole. The next thing you know, I was designing a new advertising and social media campaign for the company."

"And?" Phoebe prompted, stabbing listlessly at the edge of a lettuce leaf.

"I just came from the candy shop. I met Nancy Langley Bergstrom and pitched her my idea. She wasn't too enthusiastic at first, but then, with me using my irresistible charm and salesmanship — plus the offer of doing the work for free — she gave in."

"Cool!" Phoebe said. "But you're doing all that work for free?"

"I've been in a bit of a creative lull lately," Ivy admitted. She pushed a bit of dumpling around on her plate, not wanting to own up to the sting of losing her biggest client. "But once I tasted that candy — and I saw all those great old vintage graphics — I was just so inspired, I went into a kind of full-tilt binge. I stayed up working all night. I couldn't stop myself."

"I can't wait to see it," Phoebe said.

"Nancy's going to build a new display in the shop, using some of the old Santa photos and Christmas cards and letters," Ivy said. "You'll have to go by the candy store and check it out."

"I'll look, but I don't dare go inside," Phoebe said. "Just the smell of that fudge could undo all my hard work. Okay, back to the farmhouse. Did your furniture arrive yet? Have you started fixing it up yet? How are the chickens?"

Ivy sighed. "Well, my furniture got waylaid — it was sent to Florida. So I've been sleeping on a mattress on the floor and making do with the kitchen table and chair the Roses' son-in-law left behind. I'm already regretting donating the rest of the old furniture to the community thrift store."

"Oh no."

"Yep. But at least I had a clean slate to start working on the house. I've been painting up a storm — one room a night — and it already looks so much fresher and brighter. And I have to admit, my real estate agent has been a lifesaver. He came over and fixed the front door lock and unclogged a sink and fixed a couple broken panes of glass."

"Wow! Ezra Wheeler did all that?"

"Do you know him?" Ivy asked.

"I know who he is. All the girls at the courthouse call him the House Hunk. How'd you get lucky enough to hook up with Ezra?"

Ivy felt herself blush. "We're not 'hooked up.' I found the farmhouse online, and he happened to be the listing agent. I'd never laid eyes on him until I pulled up to Four Roses and he was waiting there with the keys."

"Pretty nice housewarming gift," Phoebe said, winking.

"It's strictly a business relationship," Ivy said. "Nothing more. I moved here for a fresh start. I'm not looking for romance."

"But it sounds to me like romance came looking for *you,*" Phoebe insisted. "I'll bet Ezra Wheeler doesn't play handyman for all his real estate clients. Anyway, what's the harm? You're single; he's single. And soooo hot."

Ivy laughed and realized, mid-giggle, that she was having fun. She was having lunch with a friend and gossiping about guys. It felt nice, and normal and . . . warm.

"You asked about the chickens? The girls are growing so fast! I've got to get their coop fixed up. That's my project this weekend."

"Need any help?" Phoebe offered. "I'm pretty handy myself. My granddad started teaching me and buying me my own power tools when I turned sixteen." She flexed a muscle. "You're looking at a lady who owns her own nail gun. And a chain saw!"

"Really? But this is such a busy time of year. You must have a million things on your own to-do list. I couldn't ask you to take on my silly henhouse."

"My shopping's all done. We put up our Christmas tree the day before Thanksgiving. I'd love to help out. Think of all the calories I could burn! Besides, I'm dying to see what you've done with Four Roses Farm."

"Well, okay, if you insist," Ivy said. "See you Saturday? And don't forget your chain saw. There's a tree growing right through the middle of my girls' chicken coop."

Chapter 10

Saturday morning's weather was sunny but cold. Ivy was sipping her second cup of coffee when the phone rang. She grabbed it when she saw the caller ID on her phone screen: Acme Movers.

"Hi? Miss Perkins? This is Stephanie at —"

"Acme Movers. I know," Ivy said impatiently. "Are you calling to tell me what time today I can expect my furniture?"

"Well . . . not exactly. I'm afraid I have some not-so-good news. You see, the truck carrying your belongings got into a bit of a fender bender in Tuscaloosa yesterday —"

"Wait. What? Tuscaloosa?" Ivy cried. "You told me my stuff was down in Florida. Tuscaloosa is not on the way to North Carolina. Not even remotely on the way —"

"If you'll just let me finish . . ." Stephanie said, sounding somewhat hostile. "Your furniture was consolidated with another load of furniture for a client in Baton Rouge. The driver was on his way back from there when he had an unfortunate collision with a log truck —"

"You just said it was a *bit* of a fender bender," Ivy interrupted. "Now it's an unfortunate collision? With a freaking log truck? Could you please just tell me what happened to my belongings?"

"The driver was able to recover a few of your pieces," Stephanie said. "He sent photos. Let's see. There's a desk lamp. What looks like a box of books. Maybe a Crock-Pot? I don't have an exact inventory yet, but I will say you might want to start shopping for a new sofa."

"My sofa?" Ivy cried. "My brand-new, blue velvet, custom-ordered down-cushioned sofa?"

"Hmm. All I have is 'blue sofa.' "

"That's it? So, you're telling me I have no furniture? At all? The only thing that survived was a six-year-old Crock-Pot that was a wedding gift from my ex-in-laws? Let me ask you something, Stephanie. You said this was 'not-so-good news.' What's your definition of good news?"

"Well, the driver escaped serious injury, and I see from your paperwork that you are fully insured. So that's what I call good news, Miss Perkins. Our claims adjuster will be in touch with you soon. Have a nice weekend."

Stephanie ended the call. Ivy looked around her chilly kitchen, barren with the exception of the chickens' crate sitting on the wooden table and the one chair she'd wisely refrained from donating to charity; then she looked down at Punkin, who was scratching at the back door, eager to greet the day. "I guess we're gonna have to go furniture shopping, buddy."

He wagged his tail.

"Right. What do you care? You've got your dog bed. All I've got is a mattress on the floor."

She opened the door and Punkin went bounding outside to greet the day.

Phoebe arrived on Saturday at nine o'clock, in a mud-spattered pickup truck, with an awe-inspiring array of power tools and an assortment of lumber. She wore a heavy plaid woolen jacket, jeans, and thick-soled work boots, and her newly blond hair was hidden under a knit ski hat.

"I wasn't sure what we'd need to fix up the chicken coop, so I just threw in some random boards and spare lumber I found hanging around in my dad's old workshop," she explained.

Ivy impulsively threw her arms around her friend. "Phoebe, this is great. I don't even know how to thank you."

Phoebe grinned. "Show me the house. I've always loved Four Roses Farm, and I'm dying to see the inside."

Ivy's own smile faded. "Not much to see, especially in the furniture department. I had a call from Stephanie with the moving company just now. The van carrying all my belongings — except for the stuff I brought up here myself — was in an 'unfortunate collision' down in Alabama. She didn't have the exact details, but it sounds like pretty much everything was destroyed."

"You're kidding! That's so awful," Phoebe said. She followed Ivy up the porch steps and paused to look out at the surrounding scenery of cedars, oaks, sycamores, and pine trees. A few late-season leaves were drifting through the cold air, and at the bottom of the hill cars moving down the county road looked like toys.

"But this view!" Phoebe said, inhaling deeply. "I can see why you fell in love with this place."

"I know," Ivy agreed. "It's so peaceful and quiet out here." She pointed toward a nearby oak. "There's an owl who must have a nest up in that tree. I hear her hooting every night. At first, I thought it was creepy. I mean, I never heard an owl in Atlanta. But now, it's sort of comforting. You know?"

Phoebe laughed. "You're such a city girl. That owl is probably hooting to her partner that she just caught a tasty field mouse for dinner."

Ivy shuddered as she opened the front door. "One less mouse to creep into my house, right?"

"It's just beautiful," Phoebe said, trailing her fingertips across the fireplace mantel after she'd toured the house. "This place is like something out of a storybook. I wish Cody and I were going to have an old farmhouse like this to move into."

"Where will you live? After the honeymoon?" Ivy asked.

"My place. It's just a crummy efficiency apartment in a complex at the edge of town," Phoebe said. "But the rent's cheap, and this way, we can start saving up a down payment for a house of our own."

"What kind of work does Cody do?" Ivy asked.

"He does something in high-tech surveillance in the Army, and he's already gotten hired to work as a mechanic at a car dealership in Asheville, but he wants to go back to night school at the technical college and get a degree in computer programming," Phoebe said. "Cody's crazy smart. He reads, like, five books a week."

"My ex and I lived in a garage apartment for the first year we were married," Ivy said wistfully. "We both had a lot of student loan debt. We couldn't even afford cable. I think that was the happiest year we spent together." She looked around at the worn wooden floors and rustic ceiling beams of the farmhouse. "I guess the lesson is, if you have love, you don't need a whole lot else."

"But a sofa would be kinda nice, right?" Phoebe joked.

"Exactly. I'm now deeply regretting my spur-of-the-moment decision to get rid of the Roses' old stuff," Ivy admitted. "It was pretty snobby of me. The woman from the moving company did say a claims adjuster will be in touch, but in the meantime, I hadn't budgeted buying this house *and* buying all new furniture. So I guess I'll have to wait for the insurance company to cut me a check."

"Hey," Phoebe said. "I still haven't met the girls."

"That's right. I moved their box into the kitchen. Right now it's the warmest room in the house."

Peep. Peep. Peepppeeeppppeeeep. The cardboard box jiggled slightly as the two women approached it. Ivy lifted the lid and pointed at the chickens, who were pecking at the feed in their dish. "That's Shirley, and that's Laverne. They're Buff Orpingtons. Those two in the corner, that's Thelma and Louise, and they're Araucanas. They're supposed to lay eggs that are blue-green."

"So cute," Phoebe said. "But you're right. They've totally outgrown this crate. I think we'd better go take a look at their new house."

Ivy gazed up at Phoebe, who was perched on a ladder beside the chicken coop. "What do you think?"

"It's not as bad as it looks," her friend reported. "There are some rotted support beams up here, but I can replace those. The main thing is that doggone mimosa tree just pushed its way up through the tin roof and peeled it back like the lid on a sardine can. I think once I cut the tree down, we can probably repair the roof."

"You make it sound so easy," Ivy said, once her friend was back on the ground. "I was afraid I'd have to hire someone to build me a whole new coop."

Phoebe patted the coop's weathered siding. "Nah. These old farm buildings were made to last. We can fix this girl up good as new again."

By noon, the mimosa tree had been sawed into neat logs and stacked at the edge of the farmhouse and Ivy had managed to conquer her fears of heights and power tools. Under Phoebe's tutelage, she sawed and nailed and screwed until her gloved hands were dotted with blisters and her back ached from climbing up and down ladders.

The two women were sitting on the porch steps, enjoying a lunch break, when the black Jeep pulled up in the driveway. Phoebe nudged Ivy. "Looks like the House Hunk is making house calls again."

As soon as Ezra Wheeler stepped out of his vehicle, Punkin bounded up to greet him, tail wagging, with a series of short, gleeful barks.

"Hey there!" Ezra called as he approached the porch. "Sounds like you've got a construction crew working. I could hear the chain saws from down at my place."

The real estate agent was dressed in worn jeans, a quilted jacket, and work boots. His beard was scruffy and his butterscotch hair ruffled in the light breeze.

"Ooh. Loving the sexy lumberjack look,"

Phoebe whispered.

"Stop!" Ivy said. She stood up, dusting off the seat of her own jeans.

"Hi, Ezra," Ivy said. "Phoebe volunteered to help me rebuild the chicken coop."

"I know you," Ezra said, reaching out to shake Phoebe's hand. "You work at the courthouse, right?"

"That's right," Phoebe said. "I see you whenever you come in to do a title search. I'm Phoebe Huddleston."

"What can I help you with, Ezra?" Ivy asked.

"Not a thing. I'm just being a nosy neighbor. Like I said, I heard all the sawing and thought I'd check it out. I'm at loose ends today. You ladies need a hand?"

"Thanks, but —" Ivy started.

"Actually, you showed up in the nick of time," Phoebe interrupted. "I was just sitting here worrying about how we're going to raise that new ridgepole for the roof with just the two of us. We need two sets of hands to hold it in place, while the third person does the nailing."

"But . . ." Ivy protested.

"I'm game if you're game," Ezra said.

Ivy had to admit the work went much faster with a third set of hands. Within an hour Phoebe and Ezra had the old roof repaired, and patched with spare sheets of tin Ivy discovered in the toolshed.

As the unskilled-labor portion of the work crew, Ivy spent the rest of the afternoon fetching tools and material, and pitching in where needed.

By four o'clock, the sun was rapidly gliding toward the western horizon as Ezra and Phoebe put the finishing touches on a new wire-enclosed run for the chickens and Ivy nailed up the old galvanized nesting boxes and spread clean straw around the floor of the coop.

"We did it," Phoebe said, stepping back to admire the refurbished henhouse. "Not bad, huh?"

"*You* did it," Ivy corrected her. She glanced over at Ezra. "The two of you, that is. I was the weak link in this outfit. I don't know how I can ever repay you. Either of you."

Ezra laughed and looked over at Phoebe. "Most of the credit goes to your job foreman. I just did what I was told."

"Teamwork makes the dream work," Phoebe said modestly. "But I wouldn't say no to something to drink."

"Oh Lord!" Ivy exclaimed. "I'm a terrible hostess. Come on inside. I've got hot cocoa, wine, and a bottle of good bourbon. I've even got a quart of eggnog in the fridge. And popcorn!"

"I should probably be going," Ezra said, but his expression said otherwise.

Phoebe gave Ivy a not-so-subtle head shake.

"Please stay," Ivy said. "Really."

"I'm just gonna put my tools back in the truck, and then I'll meet you two inside," Phoebe said, turning back to the construction site.

Chapter 11

"Want me to grab some firewood?" Ezra asked as they approached the front porch.

"Good idea," Ivy said. "I had no idea old houses could be this cold. And drafty."

She held the front door open as he entered with an armful of logs.

"My house is probably about the same age as this one, and I can tell you from experience, you probably don't have much in the way of insulation here. Last year was my first winter living there, and I thought I'd freeze to death," Ezra said. "The first thing I did with the commissions from my first few closings was invest in a heat pump and blown-in insulation."

He pushed the fireplace screen aside and arranged the logs. "Got any kind of kindling?"

Ivy pointed to a worn basket she'd retrieved from the toolshed. It was full of twigs and pine cones she'd scavenged around the property. "Here you are. I'm just gonna go fix drinks. What would you like?"

"Did somebody mention bourbon? Rocks. No water, please."

By the time she returned with his drink, Ezra had the fire blazing.

"Here you go. Sorry about the jelly jar. Good thing I didn't get rid of all the Roses' kitchen stuff."

Ezra sipped his drink. "Good bourbon tastes great no matter how you serve it." He smiled at her over the rim of his glass. "Especially with present company."

Ivy felt herself blushing again but smiled back, then took a sip of her own drink. Jelly jars, she decided, weren't all that bad.

He stood with his back to the fireplace, looking around the empty room. "I guess you city girls go for the minimalist look?"

"Not really. The moving company called this morning with the 'not-so-good news' that all my furniture was destroyed. In a fender bender. In Tuscaloosa."

"For real?"

"Yeah. The other not-so-good news is that although I have insurance, I'll have to wait for their claims adjuster to file the paperwork before I can replace what I lost. And who knows how long that will take?"

"That sucks big-time," Ezra said.

"Especially since I gave away a whole houseful of perfectly good stuff just a week ago."

"I could check with the thrift store. It's not like they have a big turnover there. Maybe you could, like, borrow the farmhouse furniture back, until you can buy stuff you really want," he offered.

"Oh, I couldn't put you to that kind of trouble . . ." she started. And then she remembered what Lawrence Jones had said earlier in the week. About it never being too late to make new friends.

"Actually, that would be wonderful," she said. "Sleeping on a bare mattress on the floor is getting old, and I'd really love to have a chair to pull up to the fire on nights like this."

"Consider it done," Ezra said. "I'll call Jake in the morning. He owes me a favor."

Ivy hesitated, then leaned in and kissed his beard-stubbled cheek. He gently placed his hand on the small of her back, so she lingered there, inhaling the scent of woodsmoke and soap.

A moment later, Phoebe burst through the front door, grinning from ear to ear, and Ivy hurriedly pulled away from Ezra.

"You guys! Come outside and look."

"What's going on?" Ivy asked as Punkin

ran out onto the front porch.

"You'll see." Phoebe jogged around the side of the farmhouse and out of sight.

It was full dark now, and it felt like the temperature had dropped by twenty degrees. Ivy wrapped her arms around her chest and shivered, and Ezra slid his arm around her shoulders.

"Ready?" Phoebe called.

"Hurry up! It's freezing out here," Ivy hollered.

"One. Two. Three!"

The porch and all the bushes and trees surrounding the house were suddenly awash in the glow of thousands of twinkling white lights.

Phoebe reappeared, looking immensely pleased with herself.

"Isn't it glorious?" she asked.

"Awesome!" Ezra said. He didn't remove his arm from Ivy's shoulder, and she didn't shrug away from him.

"Did you do all that? While we were inside lighting the fire and making drinks?" Ivy asked.

"No! I was putting my tools in the truck, and I noticed all the Roses' old lights were still strung on all the bushes and trees, and even the porch railings," Phoebe said. "I found an extension cord in your toolshed and plugged 'em in — just to see if they still worked. And they do! It's like a Christmas miracle."

"I never paid any attention to these lights out here," Ivy said. "I just assumed they were all burnt out. I mean, the house hasn't been lived in for years, right?"

"Santa Bob died while I was still in high school," Phoebe agreed. "I think Betty Rae lived a few years after that, but I can't remember the last time the house was all lit up like this."

Ivy stood at the edge of the porch and looked out over the yard. Every single shrub was draped with twinkling lights, lending the scene a fairy-tale appearance. The bare branches of tall trees were illuminated with the lights, and the farmhouse itself was outlined in lights.

"Hey, look!" Phoebe pointed down the driveway, where, at the bottom of the hill, three cars had pulled off onto the shoulder of the road. Backlit by their vehicle's headlights, the drivers stood on the roadside, pointing up at the house.

"Looks like the Fantasy of Lights is back on at Four Roses Farm," Ezra remarked.

"It really is pretty special, isn't it?" Ivy said.

"You'll leave the lights on, then?" Phoebe

asked. “At least until Christmas?”

“Yeah,” Ivy said, “I guess it won’t hurt to leave them on.”

Chapter 12

The storm started sometime after midnight. She could hear the wind howling outside, whistling down through the chimney and rattling every pane of glass in the living room and in her bedroom. Then she heard the sound of something pelting the tin roof. Pine cones? Errant Christmas lights?

Ivy shivered and burrowed deeper under the thick layer of quilts she'd piled onto her makeshift bed and was grateful when Punkin, also disturbed by the raging storm outside, arranged himself beside her on the mattress.

She was bone-tired from the day's physical exertion — up and down ladders, back and forth from Phoebe's truck to the chicken coop for tools and supplies. Her arms and shoulders ached, yet she was unable to sleep. She kept thinking of the warmth of Ezra Wheeler's arm around her shoulders, the light pressure of his palm on the small of her back when she'd impulsively leaned in to kiss him.

Was this a thing? she wondered. With Ezra Wheeler? She'd told Phoebe she wasn't looking for romance. Not interested in falling in love again. For Ivy, being in love meant being vulnerable to pain and betrayal. And that, she'd had quite enough of, thank you very much. Despite her steely resolve to erase Kyle from her memory bank, she found her thoughts wandering to her ex. He'd be spending his first Christmas with Bianca, his new bride, in the home where he'd shared the previous four holidays with Ivy.

Maybe they'd be sitting by the fireplace in the gray brick bungalow in Midtown Atlanta that she and Kyle had bought and restored together. Their Christmas tree would be aglow with lights and festooned with all the heirloom vintage ornaments from Kyle's family that Ivy had lovingly packed away the previous year, unaware that it would be the last time she would do so.

But no, Ivy thought. It was past midnight. They'd be in bed. Together, in the master suite she and Kyle had carved out of the bungalow's attic space. But the fireplace there might be burning. . . .

Ivy pulled the quilts over her head and

repeated the mantra she'd taught herself during the torturous, futile months of the unraveling of her marriage. "What doesn't kill you makes you stronger. . . ."

Punkin must have sensed her sadness. He placed his warm muzzle against her collarbone and gave it just one delicate lick.

"Good boy," she murmured, scratching his head. "I feel stronger already."

Ivy awoke to a landscape covered in snow. She pulled on another pair of socks and her boots and went out to the kitchen to boil water for coffee.

"Look, Punkin!" The dog was scratching at the kitchen door, eager to get outside. He'd never seen snow before, and it seemed to suit him just fine, as he raced excitedly across the backyard, barking his approval.

"Chickchickchickchick!" Ivy called, opening the door to the chicken coop. Her girls came running toward her, chirping excited greetings, pecking at the feed she spilled onto the floor.

"Everybody have a good night in your new house? I'm glad I put out some extra straw for you. Did you girls huddle up together to stay warm?" She filled their water dish with fresh water and poured chicken mash into their feeder.

"Okay, stay warm, ladies." Ivy dashed for the kitchen door with Punkin at her heels, her breath making clouds in the chilly morning air

She shed her damp boots, jacket, mittens, and knit cap and poured herself a cup of the coffee she'd brewed before going out to check on her flock.

"I feel like a real farmer girl," she confided in Punkin, who seemed puzzled that she was still in her pajamas — although with a sweatshirt pulled over them for warmth. "Do you feel like a farm dog? Maybe, in the spring, I should get you a cow to herd?"

Ivy stood, staring out the kitchen window at the winter wonderland that had transformed the landscape overnight. Footprints — hers and Punkin's — were the only things marring the thick white layer of snow covering everything in sight.

Snow! That sound she'd heard in the middle of the night was sleet, turned to snow. It blanketed the hard-packed ground, the weathered toolshed; even the newly rebuilt chicken coop was covered with snow. She'd been living in Atlanta — where it snowed only rarely — for so long that she hadn't considered how frequently snow came to the mountains of North Carolina.

She heard the crunch of tires on the gravel

driveway.

Punkin stood at the front door, barking furiously and wagging his tail. There were two vehicles. Ezra was emerging from his Jeep, and the box truck from the community thrift store pulled up alongside with Ezra's friend Jake at the wheel.

It was only nine o'clock. On a Sunday morning. She didn't know whether to be alarmed or grateful for her real estate agent's dogged helpfulness.

Ivy ran to the bedroom and hastily stepped out of her flannel pajama bottoms and into a pair of jeans. She ran a brush through her sleep-tangled hair. She was halfway to the front door but turned around, bolted back to the bathroom, washed her face, and brushed her teeth.

The two men staggered under the weight of the massive, lumpy sofa as they lugged it up the porch steps and into the house.

"How on earth did you manage this? On a Sunday? This close to Christmas?" Ivy asked as Ezra nodded a greeting.

"Don't ask," Jake grumbled as he set the sofa down in the same exact spot he'd moved it from only a week earlier.

"I found his mother-in-law a new house. Three hours away," Ezra said. "No more

Sunday drop-in visits from Big Mama. He owes me. Big-time."

"Consider that debt paid," Jake said. He looked around the living room. "What next? You want the dining room table and chairs?"

"All of it, I guess," Ivy said. "Especially the bed frame. And whatever else the thrift store didn't sell."

"It's all out in the truck. Every dad-burned stick of it," he added meaningfully.

"Jake?" Ezra's voice sounded a warning. "We haven't closed on Big Mama's house yet. You might want to adjust your attitude."

"I'm going." Jake trudged out onto the porch, with Punkin bringing up the rear.

After she'd tipped Jake heavily, despite his halfhearted protests, she and Ezra watched the truck pull away from the farmhouse.

"I can't thank you enough," Ivy said. "Hauling all that stuff off — and then bringing it back on a Sunday — when you could be watching football, or, I don't know, doing Christmas stuff . . ."

"Too early in the day for football. Anyway, I'm more of a pro baseball fan, myself," Ezra said. He plopped down on the sofa, looked up, and patted the cushion next to him. "Come on, sit down for a minute. Every time I come over here, it seems like you're in a constant state of motion. Don't you ever slow down?"

"I do," she protested. "How about you at least let me fix you some coffee or something?"

Ezra looked dubious.

She sank down onto the sofa beside him. "Okay, maybe you're right. It's part of my nature. I've always had a lot of pent-up energy. My grandmother used to call me Busy Lizzie. And it was high on the list of my ex's very long list of 'things I hate about Ivy.' "

"No offense, but your ex sounds like a dick," Ezra said.

Ivy guffawed. "You know what? He really *is* a dick. I've wasted *so* much time this past year, beating myself up for being a failure as a wife, for not being what he needed me to be, I guess it didn't occur to me until very recently that actually the divorce probably wasn't all my fault."

"Glad I could help out with that," Ezra said modestly. "All part of being a full-service real estate agent." He gazed around the room, at the worn but sturdy furniture, the wing chairs with their faded floral upholstery flanking the fireplace, the oak dining room set with its scarred tabletop and old-fashioned wobbly chairs, and the massive carved-oak sideboard.

"I'm sorry all your belongings got ruined in that wreck, but I gotta say, this stuff just looks like it's supposed to be here."

"You might be right," Ivy agreed. "I think it's starting to grow on me."

"There's only one thing missing," he said.

"What's that?"

He got up and walked to the right of the fireplace, to a small nook lined with bookshelves.

"You need a Christmas tree. And this is the exact right spot for it."

"What for?" Ivy countered. "It's just me and Punkin. And I've still got so much I want to do to get settled here, a messy Christmas tree is the last thing I need."

Ezra clutched at his heart, pretending to be shocked. "Do you even realize where you're living? Christmas tree farms — especially ones that sell Fraser firs — are a major part of the economy in this part of the state. According to the Tarburton Chamber of Commerce, of which I am a proud member, everyone needs a Christmas tree." He pointed down at the scarred floorboards. "Look. There are gouges in the wood here, and there's an old water stain. And there's an electrical outlet right here. I'll bet you money, this is where the Roses put up their tree.

"Maybe next year," Ivy said. Why was everyone so insistent that they knew what was good for her? "Come on out to the kitchen. The least I can do after all your hard work is give you something to drink."

Ezra wrapped his hands around the mug of coffee and leaned down to scratch Punkin's ears. "Have you guys been out playing in the snow yet?"

"Punkin went romping around a little bit this morning when we went out to feed the chickens, but it was so cold, we came right back inside," Ivy said. "I was just standing in here looking out at it when you and Jake pulled up with the furniture. It's so beautiful, all that clean, untouched white. I hate to muddy it up any more by tromping around in it."

"That's what snow's good for," Ezra said. "Besides, there's more where this came from. I saw the weather forecast this morning. We're supposed to get another two or three inches by midweek."

Ivy hesitated. "Want to take Punkin and me out for a walk in the snow? This is his first time, and I haven't seen any in years and years."

"What are we waiting for?" Ezra asked. He pointed down at Ivy's suede boots with the fake fur cuffs and looked askance. "Are those waterproof?"

"No," Ivy said, laughing at herself. "These are my city girl boots. Just give me a minute and I'll change into the same work boots I was wearing earlier."

"Okay, I'm all ready to go snowshoeing," she announced five minutes later.

But Ezra was frowning down at his phone. "I'm afraid you're gonna have to give me a rain check. I just got a call from my broker. We've got a client who's only in town for the afternoon and wants to see one of my listings. I'd try to put the guy off, but my broker insists this client is a hot prospect. It's sort of a command performance."

Ivy tried to shrug off her disappointment. "No worries. I totally understand. And like you say, there'll be plenty more snow later in the week."

"Right!" he said, brightening. "Next time it snows, lace on your boots and get ready for walking in a winter wonderland. I'm totally your guy for that."

"It's a date," Ivy promised. "In fact, maybe Punkin and I will just go for a walk by ourselves."

"Wait. I've got a better idea," he said. "The Christmas Stroll is Wednesday night. You should come."

"What's a Christmas Stroll?"

"A cynic would say it's an excuse for all the businesses in town to make one last push before Christmas. It's a town tradition. All the downtown shops stay open late and a lot of them set up booths or food carts around the square. There's caroling, and a bonfire, all that Norman Rockwell Americana stuff. Then the big moment of the night is when Santa Claus arrives on a fire engine."

"Santa, huh? Anybody I might know?"

"Afraid so. The guy who's been playing him for the past three years slipped on some ice and broke his leg last week. My broker volunteered me to be the stand-in."

"That broker of yours sounds pretty pushy," Ivy said.

"Very pushy," he agreed. "But she gets things done. So what do you say? Want to meet me on the square? We could have an early dinner and walk around and see the sights before I have to duck out and change into my outfit for the big reveal."

"Oh, I don't know," Ivy said. "I've got so much to do around here. I'm on deadline for a project for a new client —"

"It's Christmas," Ezra said firmly. "Take the night off. This is a community-wide celebration. Don't you want to become a part of Tarburton?"

"It's not that," she started to protest.

"Good. Then it's settled. I'll see you Wednesday night. Six o'clock. By the clock tower on the square."

"Okay," Ivy said.

She stood in the doorway and watched the black Jeep as it disappeared at the end of the driveway. Punkin nudged her leg. "Okay," she relented, looking around for his leash. "You're right. Let's go mess up some of that pristine white snow."

Chapter 13

Ivy couldn't believe her eyes. A small crowd was gathered on the sidewalk in front of the display windows at Langley Sweets.

"Look, Wendell." A middle-aged woman was pointing at the black-and-white photographs that were strung from festive red ribbons in the front window. "That's me, when I was six, with Santa Claus. I was asking him for a pair of Rollerblades." The woman's teenage son didn't look impressed. "Can we get some candy?" the kid asked. "Like, some fudge?"

An older married couple leaned in to get a better look at the photos. "Doesn't that look just like Mary Anne? That was the year Santa brought the kitten."

Ivy tied Punkin's leash to the bike rack on the sidewalk and edged her way into the crowded shop.

Nancy Langley Bergstrom was bustling around behind the shop's counter, weighing customers' purchases while a teenage girl rang up an order from one of the six customers lined up inside the store.

She looked up when the shop's door chimes tinkled and smiled when she caught sight of Ivy.

"Hey there!" she called. "Can you believe this?"

" 'Tis the season," Ivy replied. "I brought some ideas for a new campaign to show you, but maybe I should come back when you're not so slammed."

"Wait!" the shopkeeper said. She scurried into the shop's back room and emerged with a beautifully wrapped box, which she handed to Ivy.

"I spent the weekend testing and tweaking some of my grandma's old recipes. Try these samples and let me know what you think."

"I'll try to come by later this afternoon," Ivy said.

As she was leaving the candy shop she heard her phone ding, signaling an incoming text message. It was from Phoebe:

Can you meet me for coffee at the diner at 11? Major dilemma! Emergency!

Ivy typed her reply:

See you then.

Ivy tucked the candy box in her shopping tote. It was just ten o'clock now. She had an hour to kill before her emergency meeting with Phoebe. Maybe she'd drop by to see Lawrence Jones and enlist his help in sampling Nancy Bergstrom's latest creations.

"What a nice surprise!" Mr. Jones exclaimed when he found Ivy and Punkin standing on his doorstep. "Come on inside!"

"I hope we're not intruding," Ivy said. "We were over at Langley Sweets, and the owner asked me to sample some new recipes she's thinking of adding to the shop's merchandise. I thought you might enjoy them."

"You know Nancy?" He looked surprised.

"I do now," Ivy said, settling into the chair opposite his, while Punkin parked himself at her host's feet.

"I was really intrigued by those Peppery-Mints you gave me. So I went home and did some research. I found Langley Sweets's website, and it was so generic and blah! Not at all representative of their product, or the brand. So I did a little tinkering, drew up a new marketing campaign, and went over to the shop and introduced myself. She liked my ideas, so she's my newest client."

"Good for you," Mr. Jones said, nodding approvingly. "I like a girl with gumption."

He looked down at the large candy box, open on his lap.

He picked up a piece of candy, popped it in his mouth, and chewed slowly.

"Say!" His eyes brightened behind the thick-lensed glasses. "It's sort of . . . lemony. But there's pepper in there. And sugar. But it's not too sweet. . . ."

He held the box out to Ivy. "Try one of these round yellow ones."

Ivy shrugged and did as he suggested. She let the candy dissolve on her tongue. "You're right," she agreed. "It's tart and sweet, with sort of herbal undertones. So different from anything else I've ever tasted."

The old man selected another candy and chewed it slowly. "My doctor would give me the dickens if he knew I was eating all this sugar. He's always fussing at me about my diet."

"You look pretty healthy to me," Ivy said.

Mr. Jones patted his stomach. "Ninety-six, and never spent a single day in the hospital." He looked over at the fireplace mantel, at the photos of his departed wife and son. "But I never thought I'd outlive almost everyone in my family."

"Same with me," Ivy said softly.

"Surely not," he protested. "A young girl like you?"

"I'm an only child. I have some cousins, but we're not close," Ivy said. "I got divorced last year."

"And your folks?" he said gently.

"My dad died three years ago. It was very sudden. Heart attack." She felt unexpected tears welling up and swallowed hard. "My mom died when I was seven." She wiped at a stubborn tear. "Right after Christmas. So maybe that's why this is not my favorite time of year. Too sad."

"But you must have lots of friends," Mr. Jones pointed out. "Like the young lady you told me about, who works at the courthouse?"

"Phoebe." Ivy nodded. "Yes, she's great. Do you know, she came out to my house on Saturday, and almost single-handedly rebuilt the chicken coop. And my real estate agent, he's been an amazing help."

She recounted the sad tale of the moving van collision and told him about her agent's valiant assistance in making repairs at the farmhouse and removing and then returning the original furniture at Four Roses Farm.

"My wife and I moved nearly a dozen times back when I was working, and we never had a real estate agent do anything like that," Mr. Jones remarked.

Ivy blushed a little.

"I've tried not to encourage it, but I do think maybe he has a thing for me," she confided.

"A thing. Is that like a crush?" Mr. Jones asked.

"Yes."

"And why wouldn't you encourage a fella like that? He's not married, is he?"

"Don't think so," Ivy said. "It's hard to explain. But he's really kind."

"Good-looking?"

She blushed again. "Yes. Okay, yeah, he's very cute."

"Then what's stopping you, for Pete's sake?"

"It hasn't even been a year since my divorce. I still feel so raw. So vulnerable. To tell you the truth, I don't want to let down my guard. I'm not ready to let a man hurt me like that again."

"Ohhhh," he said, nodding. "It's like that? With your ex-husband?"

"Yes."

"I'm guessing he cheated on you?"

Ivy gulped. She took a deep breath. She hadn't told a single soul about the level of Kyle's betrayal. The loss had been too searing, too personal. And stupid.

"Yes. Kyle and I — that's my ex — we

owned a big marketing and public relations firm in Atlanta. The largest in the Southeast. Our most important client owned several high-end restaurants. Kyle and I became really close friends with the owner. Bianca. She was looking to expand into some new markets — Houston and Dallas and Birmingham. It was my account, but Kyle volunteered to help out on the project, scouting new restaurant locations, which meant lots of business trips. The next thing I know, he tells me he's deeply unhappy in our marriage. Wants time to think and 'fire himself.' That's the short version of what happened."

"I'm guessing when he found himself he found himself in love with this Bianca person?"

"Can you believe I was actually shocked?" Ivy asked.

"You trusted him," Mr. Jones said.

"And her. She'd become my best friend. I'm the one who drove her to the hospital and stayed with her when she got her boob job!"

"Oh my." The old man's cheeks bloomed a bright red.

"Sorry." Ivy laughed. "Too much information. I don't know why I'm spilling all this tea."

"Excuse me?"

"Telling you my darkest secrets. I didn't even tell my therapist this part."

Mr. Jones looked around the small living room. "It's not like I'm going to spill the tea you just spilled," he said. "I'm more or less confined to the house these days. My biggest excitement is when my neighbor takes me grocery shopping, or I have a doctor's appointment."

"You must have a very nice neighbor," Ivy said.

"I surely do. There are lots of nice folks living in this town. And it sounds to me like this real estate agent is one of them. Maybe you should give him a chance to prove it to you."

The old man's pale blue eyes twinkled from behind his glasses.

"Maybe I will," Ivy relented. "He wants to take me to dinner Wednesday night, before the Christmas Stroll."

"You must go," Mr. Jones insisted. "The Christmas Stroll is the best night of the year in Tarburton. My Polly and I used to take Ev when he was a kid. We'd have hot chocolate at the bonfire. I used to sneak a little flask in my pocket to add some Christmas cheer."

"We'll see," Ivy said. She glanced at her watch. "Oops. Better go. I'm meeting

Phoebe at the diner."

He struggled to his feet. "It was such a treat to see you today, Ivy. Please come back anytime. And thank you for the candy. You can tell Nancy Bergstrom for me that she hit a home run with all those new flavors."

"I'll do that," Ivy said. She looked over at Punkin, who was still lounging on the floor by the old man's chair. "It just occurred to me. I can't take Punkin into the diner, and it's really too cold to leave him tied up outside for more than a few minutes. Would it be okay if he stayed here with you? I won't be more than an hour."

"It would be my pleasure," Mr. Jones said, beaming.

Phoebe was clearly in a state. She was paler than usual, with dark circles under her eyes.

"What's wrong?" Ivy asked, sliding into her side of the booth.

"It's Cody," Phoebe blurted. "He called last night. He's back in the states already!"

"But that's good news, right?" Ivy asked.

"No! It's terrible. I wasn't expecting him to get back in the states this early. I still need to lose another ten pounds. I've been starving myself, but nothing's happening." She nibbled at her cuticle. "This is a disaster. I didn't sleep at all last night, and I've been like a zombie at work. I'm just going to have to tell Cody I can't see him yet."

Ivy reached across the table and grabbed her friend's hand. "Listen to me, Phoebe. You are a beautiful girl. Inside and out. You have those gorgeous dark eyes — and those lashes of yours, they're like Bambi's. You're smart and you're kind, and you're loyal, and that's what Cody must love about you."

"No." Phoebe shook her head. "You don't understand. Cody doesn't know the real me, because I've been lying to him."

"About what?"

"Everything!" Phoebe wailed. She covered her face with her hands. "All of it. It's all a lie. And now he's going to see the real me, and when he does, he'll break it off. And it's all my fault."

"Whoa," Ivy said. The waitress paused by their table with the coffeepot poised, but Ivy quickly waved her away.

"Come on, now. It can't be all that bad. So you told him a fib about your weight or something? Big deal. If he's the man you say he is, he won't care about that."

Phoebe lowered her hands. Her face was red and splotchy and tear streaked. "Cody didn't fall in love with the real me. He fell in love with a photo of some random girl I found online. She's got long blond hair and she's about a size six. I think she's a model in Sweden or something."

"Oh." Ivy was speechless.

"I know, right?" Phoebe blew her nose on a paper napkin. "I can see from your expression that you're disgusted with me. And you're right. I am pond scum. Lying to a man serving our country. Totally despicable."

"You're not pond scum, and I'm not disgusted with you," Ivy said mildly. "But what are you going to do?"

"The only thing I can do. I'm going to break it off. I'll think of a reason. Maybe tell him I'm joining a convent. Or that I have leprosy."

Phoebe's face brightened for a moment. "I could tell him I've got the flu. I'm infectious! Put off seeing him for another week or so. Just until I've lost the last ten pounds."

The waitress returned with the coffeepot and Ivy held out her mug. She waited until the server had moved on to the next table.

"Do you really want a relationship that's based on a lie?"

"Yes!"

Ivy fixed her with a stern stare.

"Okay, maybe not. But I don't know what else to do. I've screwed everything up, and I know I'm going to lose him."

"How about just telling him the truth?"

"No." Phoebe reached for a napkin from the tabletop dispenser because the tears were flowing again. "I can't face him. I'm so ashamed and embarrassed." She took her phone from her pocketbook. "He's called me twice already this morning. He sent flowers to me at the office! The most beautiful potted poinsettia."

"Call him back," Ivy said firmly. "It's time to face the music. Even if it's humiliating. You owe him the truth. A man that sends you flowers at work — that's a man worth keeping. Worth fighting for. Once he meets you in person, he'll see the real you. He'll fall in love with you all over again, because you're way better than some skinny blond Swedish bitch."

Phoebe laughed despite herself. "You're crazy, Ivy Perkins."

"I'm right and you know it."

Her friend's eyes widened. "Hold on. I've got an idea. *You* could meet Cody. You could explain it to him better than I could. I bet you could make me sound better than I really am."

"No. Absolutely not."

Phoebe reached across the table and grasped both of Ivy's hands in hers. "It's the only way. Please? Just meet Cody. Talk to him. Try to make him understand why I did what I did. And then, if he wants to break up, I won't blame him a bit."

"That's a terrible idea," Ivy said. "I'm a total stranger. Why would he listen to me? Anyway, you're just avoiding the inevitable."

"Please? I can't face him yet. Cross my heart, I will. But I just need a couple more days to get up my courage. You're older than us. Like a big sister, almost. It won't seem so crazy coming from you."

Ivy sighed. "Okay. I'll do it."

CHAPTER 14

"These are all so great — so much fun, if I didn't know better, I'd think this was some other candy company's public relations campaign!" Nancy Bergstrom leaned on the glass candy counter and leafed through the written proposal Ivy had created.

"This one — with the little red devil and the 'Sinfully Sweet' — is adorable, but I also love the Valentine's Day 'Sweeter than Kisses' one too," Nancy said. "Oh, and I love, love, love the ads about 'Treat Yourself Tuesdays. And Thursdays.' "

"One thing I think you have to do is emphasize that your product isn't just for Christmas. It's a year-round pleasure. And since your target market is mostly women, we want our customers to know that they don't have to wait for a man to buy them candy."

"Right." Nancy nodded, then sighed. "But I can't afford advertising like this, Ivy. The only reason I've been able to keep up with the bare minimum of marketing is because my mom left me this building. And the business."

"We're going to start by building you a social media profile," Ivy said. "That's free. We'll put one of these cute posters in the shop and ask your customers to follow you on your social media. If they tag you, they can be entered into a drawing to win a box of candy. Every morning, you'll style up a cute package of your candy, snap a photo, and post."

"I have an Instagram account," Nancy said proudly.

"With seventeen followers," Ivy noted. "And you haven't updated it since when? Last Mother's Day? Let me ask you something, Nancy. Do you have any customers who are sort of famous? Or somebody who's really active on social media? What we call an influencer?"

The candymaker scrunched up her face in concentration. "What's the name of the blond girl who was in that teenage slasher movie series?"

"You mean Harlowe Banks?"

"Yes!" Nancy snapped her fingers. "She has a cabin here, up on Raccoon Ridge. I think her mother grew up locally. Anyway, she comes in mostly in the summer, always wears a baseball cap and dark glasses, but one of my high school kid helpers recognized her. She loves our dark chocolate sea salt caramels and the red-hot chewies. She calls up and has me ship them to her at her home in L.A. all the time. I think she must give them as gifts."

Ivy was busy checking Harlowe Banks's social media on her phone. "OMG! She has one-point-two million followers on Instagram. Okay. Here's what we're gonna do. We'll style up a photo of the chewies with a post that says: 'Who has the hots for our red-hot chewies?' And then we'll tag her, and use the hashtag #redhotsforhotties."

"You don't think she'll mind?" Nancy said, looking doubtful.

"Better to ask for forgiveness than permission," Ivy said. "If she complains, let her know the business is in trouble and you might have to close if things don't pick up. And in the meantime, overnight her one of your Christmas assortments. Include a note thanking her for being such a loyal customer."

"What if she says no?" Nancy asked.

"But what if she says yes?" Ivy shot back. "My first boss always told me, 'You don't ask, you don't get.' "

"Okay, I'll do it," Nancy said, a slow smile spreading across her face. "You really are a marketing genius, Ivy. Since I put up that window display, business has gone crazy. I had a two-thousand-dollar day today. Two thousand! That's more than I did for all of last month. In one day!"

"I'm glad," Ivy said, glancing down at her watch. "Oops. I'd better dash. I left Punkin with Lawrence Jones an hour and a half ago. He loved all the candies, by the way."

"He's such a sweetheart," Nancy said. "Give him a hug from me."

Ivy was almost out the door. "Wait!" Nancy called. "I forgot to check. Were you by any chance coming to the Christmas Stroll on Wednesday?"

"I'm not sure. Why?"

"I've signed up for a booth on the square, but Karly, who was supposed to help work that night, just told me she's performing with the high school chorale. It's always the biggest night of the year for me, in terms of sales, and there's no way I can handle it all by myself. I was hoping maybe . . ."

"You want me to work the booth?" Ivy was taken aback.

"Never mind," Nancy said hastily. "That was way out of line. I don't know what came over me —"

"What would you need me to do?" Ivy asked. "I've never worked retail. I'd probably be more of a nuisance than a help."

"If you could help ring up sales, that would be awesome," Nancy said. "I only offer six of our most popular Christmas assortments during the stroll. They're already packaged, so there's no weighing or wrapping. I'd handle the cash sales and make change. You'd have one of my iPads, so you could run the credit sales."

"Well . . ."

"It's okay," Nancy said, shrugging. "You've been so generous to me already. I've still got three days to figure something out."

"If you can find somebody else, great. If not, then yeah, I'll do it."

The candymaker threw her arms around Ivy. "I swear, you must be the Christmas miracle I was praying for."

"You might not think so if I end up messing up all your candy sales," Ivy warned with a smile.

Punkin was sprawled on the floor in front of Lawrence Jones's armchair. "Come on, boy!" Ivy called. "Time to go home, Punkin!"

The dog raised his muzzle and yawned.

"Punkin!" she repeated.

Nothing.

"What have you done to my good boy?" Ivy demanded of the old man. "You've bewitched him."

His eyes twinkled with amusement. "I had a little hamburger left from the dinner my neighbor brought me, which I shared with Punkin. A minor bribe, that's all."

"I should sue you for alienation of affection."

Mr. Jones rubbed the dog's silky ears. "We've had a nice afternoon. I took a nap and he took a nap. I let him out in the backyard, which is fenced, and he had a grand time chasing the squirrels while I had a grand time watching."

Ivy nudged the dog's side with the toe of her shoe. "Speaking of time, it's time for us to go."

"Already?"

"We'll come again soon, I promise," Ivy said, leaning down to snap the leash on Punkin's collar.

"How did your meeting with Nancy Bergstrom go?" Mr. Jones asked, showing her to the door.

"It went really well. This is going to be such a fun account to work on. And actually, I sort of said I might help her out at the Christmas Stroll."

"Might?" He frowned. "I thought you had a dinner date with your real estate agent on Wednesday."

"I haven't confirmed that yet," Ivy said. "Anyway, he's playing Santa that night, so if I did agree to dinner, it would have to be earlier."

"Make the date," Lawrence urged. "You moved here for a fresh start, right? Take a chance. Okay?"

Punkin pulled at his leash. He was ready to go home. "Okay," Ivy said, relenting. "I'll do it."

Chapter 15

By Tuesday morning, Phoebe was in full meltdown mode, texting in all caps, with exclamation points and weeping emojis:

OMG! HE WANTS TO MEET ME TOMORROW NIGHT. HELP!

Ivy sighed and set aside her bowl of oatmeal. She picked up her phone and texted back:

This is silly. Just meet him. Explain what happened. If he's really worthy of you, he'll understand.

She looked down at Punkin, who was sniffing around the kitchen's baseboards. "Be glad you don't have opposable thumbs, pal. No texting for you."

The series of bubbles on her phone meant her friend was typing a reply:

I really can't meet him, even if I wanted to, which I don't! He wants to meet me as soon as I get off work, but Gran volunteered me to work at the church's hot cocoa and cookie booth during the Christmas Stroll. No way I can get out of it. Please???

Ivy took a last spoon of oatmeal. The bottom of the bowl revealed the faded figure of a painted reindeer. The bowl's glaze was crazed and browned with age, but the edge of the bowl was festooned with a pattern of red and green holly leaves. It was part of a set of seven bowls she'd found in the farmhouse kitchen cupboard, along with six matching plates and four chipped mugs. The Rose family had taken Christmas very seriously. She'd also discovered a set of vintage Twelve Days of Christmas tumblers in the dining room hutch.

Each piece of the china depicted a different woodland creature: a rabbit, a fox, a squirrel, a perky redbird, and even a wise old owl. She was grateful there was no mouse to remind her of the scratching sounds she'd been hearing from the vicinity of her attic.

Before moving to Four Roses Farm, Ivy Perkins would have considered the china kitschy, even tacky, but here, in this rustic setting, with the sun shining in through the wavy glass windows, Ivy decided the dishes were charming.

Her phone dinged to remind her that she hadn't answered her friend's last text.

Please????

Ivy sighed and started to type:

What's the plan?

She was still shaking her head over Phoebe's screwball scheme when she heard the crunch of tires on the driveway.

Punkin heard it too and bounded, barking, toward the front door. By the time Ivy joined her dog, the doorbell was ringing. When she opened the door she found Ezra Wheeler standing on her porch, holding a towering Christmas tree in one leather-gloved hand. He looked incredibly pleased with himself.

Ivy was momentarily speechless. "What . . ."

"Look, I know you said you didn't need a tree, but I just don't think it's right to spend your first Christmas at the Four Roses farmhouse without a tree. And this one was free! I cut it down myself. My place used to be a Christmas tree farm, back in the day, and the former owner left a small stand of older trees at the back of my property. I've been thinning them out, thinking I'll get around to planting some new trees. . . ."

"It's beautiful," Ivy said finally. "But it's really, really big, isn't it? Will it even fit in my house?"

"Oh sure," he said. "You've got ten-foot ceilings here. Want me to bring it in and set it up for you?"

She held the door open and stepped aside as he dragged and shoved the tree through the doorway and into the living room. The room was immediately filled with the scent of fresh-cut evergreen, as he leaned the tree against the fireplace.

He went back out to the porch and handed her a paper bag. "That's a special plug with a built-in timer for all the outdoor Christmas lights. I'll set it up before I leave. That way, every night they come on automatically."

He pointed at the fireplace nook. "I think you should put the tree over there, where the Roses put theirs," Ezra said.

"Be my guest."

He dragged the tree toward the nook near the fireplace, then looked around expectantly. "Christmas tree stand?"

Ivy laughed despite herself. It was such a man thing to do. Show up, unannounced, with a Christmas tree, but no stand.

"I don't have one."

"Oh." He looked around the room. "You sure? I mean, the family left almost everything else. You sure there's not a Christmas tree stand stashed somewhere around here?"

"I haven't seen one, but since I didn't plan on getting a tree this year, I haven't really gone looking."

"I've probably got a spare out in the barn at my place," he said. "I can drop it by later, and help you get the tree set up in it, if you want."

Ezra's hopeful grin, his pure boyish enthusiasm for life, Ivy decided, was irresistible.

"That'd be fine. But you'll have to stick around to help decorate it too."

"You got a deal," he said. "And, uh, I've got a favor to ask."

"What's that?"

"You know I told you my boss drafted me into playing Santa tomorrow night? Well, she dropped the old guy's Santa suit off to me this morning, and I gotta say, it's *no bueno.*"

"What's wrong with it?"

"I've got it out in the Jeep. Hang on and I'll show you."

He was back a moment later, holding a plastic garment bag. He draped the bag on the back of the sofa and unzipped it.

The suit was made of some kind of flimsy shiny polyester fabric that had once been red but was now faded almost to coral. He held it up so she could examine it. It was trimmed with yellowing cotton batting and the jacket was fastened with Velcro strips.

"Wow. That's really awful," Ivy said. "Plus it looks so flammable it could spontaneously combust at any moment."

"I think the old Santa was more like a gnome," Ezra added. "The pants barely hit below my knees, and I couldn't get the jacket fastened across my chest. At all."

Ivy guessed at the favor he was about to ask.

"Why don't you just wear Santa Bob's old suit? It's a shame to just leave it sitting in my closet."

"I was hoping you'd say that."

She retrieved the box and set it on the living room sofa and handed him the jacket. "Better try it on."

Ezra slid his arms into the sleeves and easily fastened the buttons. He pulled the excess fabric away from his chest. "Wow. I never met Santa Bob, but I'd say he was a pretty husky fellow."

"That's easily fixed," Ivy said, handing him the pants.

He held out the waist of the pants to demonstrate how roomy they were.

"But the length looks right," Ivy said. "I think you tuck the legs into the boots."

Ezra easily pulled the pants of the Santa suit over his own jeans. "I'm gonna have to either start carb-loading before tomorrow night, or get somebody to alter these."

"Let me see," Ivy said. She tugged at the waist of the red velvet pants and noticed a drawstring casing on the inside of the waistband.

"Look here," she said. "You can adjust them with this drawstring. Pretty clever."

"I'm still swimming in this thing," he protested.

"Stay right there," she said, retreating to the bedroom. When she returned she held out a pillow.

"Here." Standing close, she tucked the pillow beneath the waistband of the red velvet pants. She stood on her tiptoes and placed the hat, with its jaunty fur pom-pom, at a rakish angle on his head, then took a half step backward. "Much better."

"Much, much better," he said. And before she could move away, Ezra put his arms around her waist and pulled her closer. "I've got a better idea. How about if you stay right here," he said, nuzzling her neck.

She gave him a quizzical look and started to say something, but then his lips found hers.

His kiss was tender, even hesitant at first, but his lips were warm and Ivy found herself responding in kind, sliding her arms around his neck and melting into his embrace with an urgency that took her by surprise.

He parted her lips with his tongue, and as she moved her hands beneath the Santa jacket she felt, then heard the buzz coming from the front pocket of his jeans.

"Nooo," he muttered. "Not now."

"Turn it off," Ivy whispered, running her hands up his bare chest. "We're busy here."

He inhaled sharply and groaned.

"Can't," he whispered as he dug in his pocket for his phone.

He looked up from the caller ID screen. "It's the boss. We've got an offer pending on my listing, but the buyer wants to close before the end of the year, which means I've got to scramble to get the contract drawn up."

"Oh."

He unbuttoned the jacket of the suit and quickly stepped out of the oversized pants, then folded the suit into the cardboard box. "Hate to kiss and run, but if I ignore her she'll just keep texting."

"It's okay," Ivy said. She stooped down to pick up the hat, which had somehow fallen off during their heated embrace, and handed it to him.

"Gonna need this."

He grinned and she felt a sizzle of electricity run down her spine.

"I'll stop by later after I get all the paperwork submitted. You know, to help get the tree set up and everything."

"Yeah." Ivy laughed, making a shooing motion. "That too."

CHAPTER 16

The longer Ivy stared at the massive Christmas tree the more she longed to get it set up, decorated, and lit. But without a stand, that was impossible. Remembering what Ezra had said about checking for a stand in his barn, she decided to check in her own toolshed.

When she went outside to search, she was shocked at how much the temperature had plummeted. Sunday night's snow had melted and then frozen, and the ground was icy and slick. The shed was full of rusty tools and mysterious-looking farm implements of all sorts, but there was nothing even remotely resembling a Christmas tree stand.

She decided to check on her hens before she returned to the house, to make sure that they were snug in their new home. She heard the chickens clucking as she approached the coop, and when she opened the door to check on them her girls came running excitedly toward her. She checked the water in their bowl, breaking the thin layer of ice on the surface, and distributed an extra cup of mash and placed fresh straw in their nesting boxes.

Her breath made frosty puffs in the air, but the chickens didn't seem bothered by the cold.

"Punkin, let's go!" she called. The setter was joyously racing around the yard, barking and romping through the remains of the snow.

He reluctantly abandoned the squirrel he'd treed and followed her back inside the house.

"The Roses must have had a Christmas tree stand," she told the dog as he lapped water from his bowl. "But the question is where? I've looked in all the closets."

The dog sat on his haunches, stuck his muzzle in the air, and whined.

Ivy looked up and for the first time noticed the rectangular door cut into the kitchen ceiling. A piece of stout rope hung down from the edge.

"I guess that's the pull-down stairs to the attic, right?"

Punkin thumped his tail.

"I think there are mice up in that attic," she said. "That's what that scratching sound we hear at night is. Mice."

He sprawled out on the floor and gave a short, enthusiastic bark.

"Just this once I wish you were a cat," Ivy told him. She sighed and reached for the rope. The hinges creaked in protest as the wooden stairs unfolded.

Ivy grabbed a flashlight and looked over at the dog. "If I'm not back in ten minutes, go find Ezra, you hear?"

She climbed the wooden stairs slowly. "Hey, mice!" she called, poking her head through the attic opening. "If you're up here, consider yourself evicted. I mean it. Head for the hills!"

Ivy turned on the flashlight and flicked it around the cavernous attic space. The ceiling was higher than she'd expected, and the space was cluttered, stacked with trunks and boxes and outdated bits and pieces of furnishings the Roses had long ago abandoned.

She pulled herself to a standing position and began looking around at what she realized must be several generations of family belongings. There were dusty cribs and dressers, a folded-up wheelchair, racks of plastic-draped clothing. She spotted a wooden rocking horse, a mahogany armoire with a mirrored door, and an old treadle-powered sewing machine that reminded her of the one her grandmother had kept in a spare bedroom.

In one corner of the slope-ceilinged space she saw a tall stack of wooden fruit crates with a hand-lettered sign: CHRISTMAS.

"Thank goodness these people were organized," she muttered. She played the flashlight over the crates and saw that they were labeled: LIGHTS, ORNAMENTS, TINSEL, GARLAND.

She flipped the top of one crate and saw what looked like hundreds of big, old-fashioned C9 colored Christmas bulbs with thick intertwined red and green electrical cords. She moved the crate aside and found another containing extension cords and an electric color wheel. A faded box behind it was labeled: ALUMINUM TREE.

"Oooh," she whispered, lifting the lid. "Awesome." She'd seen retro stores in Atlanta selling trees like this for over a hundred bucks. Maybe when Ezra came back he'd help her take the tree downstairs. It might be fun to set it up on the porch.

On the floor behind the aluminum tree she spotted her prize. A rusting red cast-iron Christmas tree stand. It was heavier than she expected, but that was good. She'd need something sturdy to keep that massive tree from falling over.

She was picking it up when she spied a large, flat box with gold wrapping paper. It had fallen off the stack of fruit crates and was wedged up against the wall. When she pulled it out of its hiding spot she saw that it too was labeled. BETTY RAE.

Ivy held her breath as she lifted the top off the box. Inside she found more yellowing tissue paper and, beneath that, a plush red velvet jacket with a white fur collar. The smell of mothballs made her eyes water momentarily.

"Hello, Mrs. Santa," she whispered.

She lifted the jacket from the box. It was beautifully tailored with a snug-fitting bodice that nipped in at the waist and flared out at the hips. The buttons were jet black and the lining was satin.

Impulsively, Ivy pulled her sweater over her head and tried on the jacket. The lining felt silky against her skin, and to her surprise, the jacket fit perfectly, almost as though it had been custom tailored for her.

She shook the skirt out from the tissue and held it up against her body. The waistband was surprisingly tiny, but the traumatic events of the past year had left Ivy with little appetite and she'd effortlessly dropped twenty pounds on what her therapist called "the divorce diet" of Tic Tacs and sauvignon blanc.

The floor-length skirt was full, with a red taffeta petticoat that rustled as she stepped into it, and one side of the fur-trimmed hem was caught up in a sort of side bustle.

She zipped herself into the skirt and did a quick twirl, loving the feel of the taffeta swishing against her ankles. Glancing into the box, she spotted two more accessories — a fur-trimmed velvet hat with a pompom, and a white fur muff with an old-fashioned corsage of silk poinsettia petals.

Ivy stood in front of the mirrored armoire and examined herself in the cloudy glass. She popped the hat on top of her hair and thrust her right hand into the muff. Her fingers touched a scrap of fabric, and when she withdrew it she saw that it was a handkerchief with a red embroidered scalloped border of poinsettias and Christmas bells. She held the handkerchief to her nostrils and was greeted with the scent of roses and the faint smell of . . . cinnamon? Cloves?

She stood, transfixed, in front of the mirror, fluffing the skirt and turning this way and that, her being suffused with an unexpected sense of warmth and calm and . . . something like peace?

Just then she heard Punkin start barking

down below in the kitchen. A voice called from the front of the house.

Ivy scrambled down the stairs as fast as she could, although her speed was encumbered by the volume of the long skirt.

"Ivy?" Someone was rapping at the front door, where Punkin was posted, barking enthusiastically and wagging his tail.

It was Phoebe. She stood on the porch, her hand wrapped around a spindly four-foot-tall evergreen — complete with a Christmas tree stand.

Her friend giggled at the sight of Ivy. "Hello, Mrs. Claus! I see you're finally getting in the spirit."

"I was up in the attic, looking for . . ." She paused, pointing at the tree. "What's that?"

"Um, it's a midsized evergreen. Fraser fir. What's it look like, silly? I know it's pushy of me, but I just couldn't stand the idea of your not having a Christmas tree. This one is kind of a Charlie Brown tree, but since it's sort of wonky, the guy at the lot sold it to me for five bucks."

"For me?" Ivy hugged her friend. "That's so sweet. And thoughtful."

"Well?" Phoebe peered around her, toward the living room. "Are we gonna stand out here in the freezing cold, or are we gonna set it up inside?"

"Doh!" Ivy smacked her forehead. "Yes, come on in. The only thing is . . ."

Phoebe set her tree just inside the doorway and pointed an accusing finger at the tree by the fireplace. "Hey! Looks like someone beat me to the punch."

"Ezra. He says his property used to be a Christmas tree farm and he's been culling some of the older trees because he wants to plant some new ones."

"The old Freeman place," Phoebe said, looking up at the tree. "Freeman's Fraser Fir Farm. It's only about a half a mile down the road from here." She gave Ivy a sly wink. "Convenient, right? And unique. Any dude can bring a girl flowers or candy. But not everyone gifts his new squeeze with a Christmas tree. And a twelve-foot-tall tree, at that."

"He's not my squeeze. He's just . . . a nice guy," Ivy said. "A really nice guy," she added. "Of course, being a guy, he didn't think to bring a stand— like you."

"I think it's a Y-chromosome thing," Phoebe said. "Cluelessness."

"He said he'd bring me a stand later, after he finishes with some deal he's trying to close before Christmas, but in the meantime, I scouted around, went up into the attic, and found a stand. Along with this," she said, gesturing at her outfit. "I was just getting ready to bring the stand down from the attic when you showed up."

"You just found that up in the attic?"

"In a gold box labeled 'Betty Rae.' I couldn't resist trying it on."

"It fits like it was made for you," Phoebe said. "But I can't believe Betty Rae Rose ever fit into that outfit. I bet she weighed at least fifty pounds more than you."

"Huh." Ivy smoothed the jacket over her hips. "Don't think I'm crazy, but I got the weirdest feeling when I tried it on."

"Like what?"

"I don't know. Just sort of warm and glowy inside, like the human embodiment of a cup of hot cocoa. I'm insane, right? Comes from living alone."

Phoebe gave it some thought. "Eccentric, maybe. But not necessarily crazy. What is crazy is that now you're apparently stuck with two Christmas trees. What should we do with my poor lil' guy?"

"Let's set it up on the front porch," Ivy said. "But first, I need to get out of this dress and bring that stand down from the attic. I found a ton more old-timey lights up there too — the ones with the big colored bulbs. Hopefully, they're not a fire hazard."

"Bring 'em down and let's get decorating," Phoebe said. "I'll give you a hand."

"Wait a minute," Ivy said. "Aren't you supposed to be at work right now?"

"I'm off work until January. This happens every year. I have days and days of paid comp time built up that I never take, because I essentially have no life." She smiled at Ivy. "Until this year."

"And Cody," Ivy said.

"Let's talk about him later. We've got trees to trim, right?"

Phoebe followed Ivy up the ladder and into the attic. Looking around, she gave a low whistle. "Look at all this stuff!"

"It's sort of sad, isn't it? When I asked James, the Roses' son-in-law, he said he and his kids just aren't sentimental. They took a few things, some photo albums, but he told me to just get rid of anything else I didn't want. At the time I was pretty annoyed, because everything here was pretty old-fashioned, and definitely not my taste, but now that it turns out all my stuff was wrecked, 'old-fashioned' seems to be growing on me. So I'm feeling pretty grateful."

"One man's trash is another man's treasure," Phoebe murmured. "There's another whole houseful of furniture up here."

"If you see anything you'd like, speak up. It's not doing anyone any good gathering dust up here," Ivy said. She pointed at the far wall. "That's the Christmas corner. Everything's labeled. Let's grab a crate of lights, and I guess we'll need an extension cord too."

When they'd returned downstairs, Ivy changed back into her jeans and sweater and carefully laid the Mrs. Santa dress across her bed. When Ezra dropped by later, she thought, maybe she'd model it for him. She pictured herself standing in front of the lit-up Christmas tree, a fire blazing, Ezra sitting in an armchair. She'd been thinking about their kiss since he'd left. Maybe one thing would lead to another?

Chapter 17

"We did it!" Phoebe stepped back from the Christmas tree in the living room and she and Ivy exchanged high fives.

Setting up the tiny tree on the front porch was a breeze, but Ezra's tree was a different story. They'd had to saw a foot off the tree trunk, then drag a ladder in from the toolshed to wrap what seemed like miles of the big, multicolored C9 lights around the fir. The silver-tinseled garland from the attic came next, followed by more of the fragile glass Shiny Brite ornaments from the Christmas corner.

The effort had taken them all afternoon. They'd stopped for lunch — homemade vegetable soup and corn muffins Phoebe's mother had sent along — but it was nearly dark by the time Ivy hung the last red and gold glittered ornament on the tree.

When she got off the ladder she glanced surreptitiously at her phone again, as she'd done several times throughout the afternoon, but there was no text message or missed call from Ezra.

He's busy, she told herself. It's just business.

"It needs something else," Phoebe said, studying their handiwork.

"A skirt," Ivy proclaimed. "And I've got just the thing."

She went to the hall linen closet and brought out a red and white calico quilt. Parts of the old fabric had worn through in places, revealing the batting, but the colors were still vivid. Kneeling down on the floor, she draped it around the base of the tree.

"Perfect," Phoebe said. "Don't tell me the family left that behind too? Betty Rae Rose was in a quilting guild with my grandmother. I'd never think of giving up one of her quilts."

"I know," Ivy said. "I found a stack of them in a cedar chest in the guest bedroom. And thank goodness I did. This place is unbelievably drafty. Ezra says I'm probably going to have to have the farmhouse insulated. And a new furnace is definitely on my must-have list, as soon as I can afford it."

" 'Ezra says,' " Phoebe teased.

"He's a real estate agent," Ivy protested. "And he knows a lot about old houses like this one."

"What else does he know a lot about?"

"You're *utterly* shameless," Ivy said, shaking her head.

"I'll take that as a compliment," Phoebe said. She pulled her phone from her pocket. "Yikes. I'd better go. I promised Gran I'd help bake cookies for tomorrow night."

"Let's talk about tomorrow night," Ivy said. "I really, really don't think your plan for me meeting Cody, instead of you, is a good idea."

"But you promised," Phoebe groaned. "It's only for a few days. Until I can get up the nerve to meet him in person and come clean about everything."

"It's unfair to him," Ivy said. "And it's dishonest."

"A promise is a promise," Phoebe said. "Anyway, you have to do it now that I helped rebuild your chicken coop and decorated not one but two Christmas trees. You owe me."

"I get it now," Ivy said, walking her friend to the front door. "You were scheming this all along. Helping out the new girl in town and then — suddenly, *boom* — it's payback time. I should have known you had an ulterior motive."

"Me?" Phoebe feigned a look of innocence. "I was just trying to be a good neighbor, that's all."

"Whatever. I'll call you tomorrow. Hopefully you'll have changed your mind. But I might have to rearrange my plans. I promised to help Nancy Bergstrom work at her candy shop booth during the Christmas Stroll. But Ezra wanted to take me to dinner early — because he got roped into playing Santa Claus during the stroll."

"Maybe you could have dinner after the Santa Claus thing? That way you could meet Cody at the clock tower at five, tell him how sick I am, and how I'm deadly contagious. And then you go sell candy with Nancy, and whisper sweet nothings over dinner to Ezra."

"You're *utterly* shameless," Ivy repeated. "Someone should have warned me about getting mixed up with somebody like you — such a terrible influence."

"One more thing," Phoebe said, turning as she walked out the door. "Wear that Mrs. Santa dress tomorrow night. That thing is magical."

Ivy stepped onto the porch and watched Phoebe pull down the driveway. The lights blanketing the trees and the house blinked on, and she stood, for just a moment, enjoying the spectacle. They'd placed Phoebe's tree to the right of the front door, and when Ivy plugged it in, the bright lights cast their reflection on the worn wooden porch floor. Looking down the sloped drive, she saw cars slow, then stop on the county road to get a better look at the lit-up farmhouse. She found herself waving and smiling at the occupants of a minivan, whose driver got out and was taking photos with his cell phone.

Then a sudden, strong gust of frigid wind drove her back inside the farmhouse.

Earlier in the afternoon, at Phoebe's suggestion, they'd tromped around the property, clipping boughs of cypress, magnolia, and red-berried holly and white tallow berries and then dragged them inside.

Now Ivy draped the evergreens and magnolia sprays on the mantel, tucking in sprigs of holly and waxy, white tallow berries among the greenery. Candles would add a nice touch, Ivy thought. She experienced a brief pang of regret, remembering the collection of sterling candlesticks she'd inherited and collected over the years. Would they be among the items salvaged from the wrecked moving van?

No wallowing in self-pity, she thought sternly, standing up and dusting off her hands as though to banish that unwelcome emotion.

She didn't need sterling silver to enjoy her new home and this moment.

There were dozens of old jelly jars in the bottom of the kitchen's Hoosier cabinet, along with a box of thick, white utility candles. She placed the candles in jars, lit them and tucked them among the greenery on the mantel, lit the fire she'd laid earlier, then sat on the sofa with a glass of wine to admire her handiwork. When Punkin jumped up to curl up alongside her, she didn't bother to shoo him off the furniture.

Ivy sipped her wine and stared at her phone again. No word from Ezra. She thought about their clinch — and that smoldering kiss they'd exchanged, much earlier in the day. He'd promised to be back later, after his client meeting. But ten hours had passed since then. Should she dash off a breezy text message — just checking in? Absolutely not. She would not play the needy female who needed rescuing.

Reheated soup and some cheese and crackers became dinner, eaten in front of the fire. Despite her earlier resolve, she found her mood darkening, found herself brooding about the past, about faithless men and their meaningless promises.

Tears pricked her eyelids, and Punkin,

always sensitive to her emotions, laid his head in her lap, gently nudging her hand until she complied with his unspoken request, stroking the top of his head, crumpling his silky ears between her fingertips, and stroking his outstretched neck.

Finally, at ten, when the setter stood patiently in front of the kitchen door, she let him outside and stood on the covered back porch, shivering and staring up at the deep blue sky, shot through with millions and millions of tiny, twinkling stars.

"Punkin, come!" she called, hearing him tearing through the underbrush. For once, he obeyed, racing back toward her, out of the freezing night air and into the warm house.

Retreating to her bedroom, Ivy stared at the Mrs. Claus dress that she'd draped across the bed. She ran her fingertips across the warm velvet fabric, then tossed it onto a nearby chair. She donned her warmest pajamas and crawled beneath the layer of quilts. Her eyelids drooped, almost as soon as her head hit the pillow. Just before she surrendered to her weariness, she heard the farm's resident owl, hooting from the highest limb of the pecan tree nearest the house.

Tires crunched on the gravel driveway.

Punkin raised his head and pricked up his ears. He heard the clump of boots on the porch steps, followed by three hesitant taps at the door. He glanced over at Ivy, whose soft, regular breaths remained untroubled. The dog stood, stretched, turned three times, then resumed his position at the foot of her bed. After a moment, the footsteps retreated.

CHAPTER 18

Ivy took one look at the ice-covered back porch and the treacherous frozen waterfall that had once been the steps leading down to the yard. "That looks like a one-way trip to the emergency room," she told her dog. "Let's try the front door."

Punkin raced ahead of her. The door stuck slightly, and when she finally managed to open it he bounded outside to relieve himself. When she looked down, she saw a package sitting on the porch floor, beside Phoebe's Charlie Brown Christmas tree.

Even without opening it, she could tell from the shape and heft that it was a bottle of some kind. It was clumsily wrapped in now-damp tissue paper, with a limp bow of red ribbon. A small card was taped to the paper. She ripped the envelope open and found Ezra's business card. There was a note on the back:

Sorry. Closing documents were a disaster. Like the rest of my day. I knocked, but you must have been asleep. Do-over? Xoxo, Ezra.

"No show, no call? No dice," she muttered.

Punkin was back, shaking himself and splattering her with icy drops of half-melted snow.

"Men!"

Ezra's gift was a bottle of Silver Oak Cabernet. It was a very, very nice wine. But it was no balm for her disappointment. She left the wine on the kitchen counter and headed for the shower. Exactly two minutes later her yelp of shock brought the dog running to her closed bathroom door, where she was just emerging, teeth chattering, from the shortest, coldest shower she'd ever endured. This time, she knew, it wasn't an empty propane tank.

"Looks like Santa's going to bring a new hot-water heater," she told the dog. "Merry Christmas to us."

The problem was, Ivy had no idea where one could obtain a hot-water heater the week before Christmas, or who to call to install one.

Luckily, Phoebe knew exactly what to do. "You need Ronnie Cahill. He does maintenance for the county public works department, but he's got a plumbing business on the side. Only thing is, you can't call him during the day. In fact, you can't call him at night either, because his wife doesn't know he's got a side hustle."

"Wait. His wife doesn't know he's a plumber?"

"She doesn't know he's working off the clock to pay under-the-table child support to his ex-girlfriend–slash–baby mama," Phoebe said. "You'll have to try and track him down in person."

Ivy's voice reflected her panic: "This can't wait another day. My hot-water heater is dead. I had icicles coming out of my showerhead this morning."

"Why don't you just call Ezra?"

"Never mind," Ivy said. "I'll figure out something."

"You two have a fight?"

"He never did call yesterday. I guess he came by the house late. I found a bottle of wine on my doorstep this morning, with a note saying he was sorry, but his closing documents were a disaster."

"Oh-kayyyy," Phoebe said. "That sounds valid. It's the guy's job, Ivy. And it's been a tough year for business around here lately. Why not cut him some slack?"

Ivy let out a long, aggrieved sigh. "If he shows up at my house with a new hot-water heater and a toolbox, maybe I will. Let's talk about tonight. Are we all set?"

"Yep. Cody texted me this morning. He's in training for his new job all day, but he'll be waiting at the clock tower on the square at five. You'll be there, right?"

"I'll be the girl wearing a hat, since I couldn't wash my hair this morning."

Ezra called at noon. Ivy held the phone and debated whether or not to pick up. Then she remembered her defunct hot-water heater.

Her tone, when she answered, was as chilly as her morning's shower.

"You're pissed," Ezra said. "And you have every right to be. But can I explain?"

"I'm listening."

"Look, I'm truly sorry. I know I should have called yesterday. But every time I picked up the phone, my broker was right there, harassing me about how we're going to keep this deal from imploding."

"And did you? Manage to salvage it?"

"Just barely. The property is an old brick textile mill just outside the county line. Our client is buying it to redevelop into multi-family residential, with some mixed-use commercial space on the ground floor. Unbeknownst to any of us, there were all kinds of nitpicky little problems with the title and the property survey that have to be worked out before we close on December 29. And guess who's in charge of unsticking all that red tape?"

"Your broker sounds like a toxic beast. I don't get why you work for somebody like that," Ivy commented, reluctantly finding empathy for him.

"She's demanding, that's for sure," Ezra agreed. "But I gotta admit she doesn't expect any more of me than she expects of herself. It's funny that you should say that, because she actually wants to meet you."

"Me? Why?"

Long silence at the other end of the line. "In the middle of everything yesterday, when things were getting pretty tense, I, uh, might have told her that, uh, I've met somebody I want to spend more time with."

Ivy was taken aback by his answer. "Why would you tell your broker about us?" she demanded.

"Can I just explain tonight? You're still going to let me take you to dinner before the Christmas Stroll, right?"

Ivy felt her resolve melting. It was time to get tough.

"I can't have dinner early, because I made a commitment to Phoebe. But I could do it later. On one condition."

"Name it."

"My hot-water heater quit this morning. And I know this time it's not just the propane. It's dead. Kaput. I'm supposed to help Nancy Bergstrom with her booth during the stroll tonight, and I cannot show my face there with janky hair."

"Ohhhhhh." He let the word hang there.

"Do you happen to know where I can get a hot-water heater? And someone who can install it? Before tonight?"

"No promises this time," Ezra said. "But I'll see what I can do. I'll call you later today. No matter what."

The black Jeep pulled into the driveway an hour later, followed by a battered white van. By the time Ivy got to the door, Ezra and another man were jockeying a new hot-water heater up the porch steps.

"That was fast," Ivy commented, holding the door open to allow them to enter.

"Ivy Perkins, meet Ronnie Cahill," Ezra said.

The plumber was middle-aged, with a

stout beer belly and a graying beard. He favored her with a curt nod. "Hey. Where's the basement at? I got a backed-up toilet at the senior center after this."

"Right this way," she said. Just before descending into the basement with Cahill, Ezra leaned in and whispered in her ear, "I'm supposed to tell you it'll be five hundred dollars. No credit card, no checks, no questions. Cash only."

"Guess I'll be making a run to the ATM in town," Ivy said. She squeezed his hand. "Thanks, Ezra."

As the van backed out of the driveway two hours later, Ivy was in the kitchen, turning on the tap. When the water gradually turned warm, then hot, she gave a happy, contented sigh before turning her attention back to Ezra.

"How did you get Ronnie Cahill here on such short notice? Phoebe told me about him, but she said he was impossible to reach on short notice, because he works for the county."

"Let's just say Ronnie and I have an understanding," Ezra said. "I helped a friend of his find a new, cheaper house on the other side of town. Instead of his paying me a commission, we traded out for plumbing. And emergency plumbing services."

"Is the friend an ex-girlfriend? And the mother of his child?"

Ezra raised an eyebrow. "I'm not at liberty to discuss my client's private affairs."

"Especially the extramarital affairs?"

"Never mind that," Ezra said. "I lived up to my end of the bargain. Does that mean you'll have dinner with me tonight?"

"I guess it does," Ivy said. "What time will you be done?"

"Santa's shift ends at eight. Can you meet me there? I'll be set up in Santaland on the square. We have an eight-thirty reservation at The Wine Cavern."

"I'll be there," Ivy said. She leaned in and kissed him lightly on the cheek.

Chapter 19

It was the best, most delicious shower Ivy had ever had, and she vowed that she would never again take hot water for granted. She was drying her hair when she glanced down at the phone on the bathroom sink and saw that she'd missed a call from Phoebe. Maybe, she thought, her friend was having second thoughts about her plan.

"Ivy? I need another favor. A big one. I'm supposed to be at the church in thirty minutes, but my car won't start. I think the battery is dead. Can you give me a ride to the square?"

"Uh, yeah. I think I can get ready by then."

"Great. I'll text you my address. Hurry, okay? If I'm late I'll be shunned by the entire Tarburton United Methodist Ladies Auxiliary."

Ivy hustled into the bedroom, trying to decide what to wear. She'd seen the weather forecast: clear and cold. So, jeans, boots, sweater, jacket, since she'd be outside most of the evening. The red velvet Mrs. Santa dress was right where she'd tossed it the night before.

Should she? After all, with the layers of lining and heavy fabric, it should be plenty warm. And she had to agree with Phoebe, the outfit really did suit her. Most important, she thought Ezra would get a kick out of seeing her wearing it. She dug into her dresser and pulled out her thickest pair of tights. As she was buttoning the jacket and adjusting the fur collar, she felt a warm glow settle over her body.

The elf was standing, shivering, in front of the address of the apartment Phoebe had texted her from. She wore a form-fitting red-and-green-striped tunic, a tall, red peaked cap, baggy yellow tights, and red booties that curled at the toes. She was holding a bulky white cardboard box.

Ivy rolled down the passenger side window. "Phoebe? Is that you?"

Her friend slid into the front seat. "Just drive, okay? I'll explain on the way to church."

"Gran made this ridiculous elf costume

when my mom was my age. Mom used to wear it every year at the Christmas Stroll. It was a way to drum up business. People would come over and have their picture taken with her, and then they'd buy cookies and cocoa for the family. It's the women's auxiliary's biggest fundraiser of the year and all the money they make goes to the church's food pantry. Anyway, after having three kids and what she calls middle-aged spread, Mom hasn't worn it in ages. But this year, since I've lost weight, Gran decided the elf costume should come out of retirement. And as my granddad used to say, arguing with Gran is like trying to fart into a tornado."

Ivy chuckled at the thought of the two of them, Mrs. Santa and an overgrown elf, driving around town in a Volvo station wagon. "You look adorable. I just hope we don't get pulled over for speeding."

"Right? By the way, I'm so glad you decided to dress up tonight too. What made you change your mind?"

"Hmm? Like you said, I thought it would be a fun way to draw business to the candy shop booth."

"Nope. I'm not buying that," Phoebe said, shaking her head.

"Okay," Ivy relented. "You're right. It was

Ezra. He called to apologize for last night, and then he showed up at my house with a new hot-water heater *and* your pal Ronnie Cahill, who installed it. How could I say no? I mean, it's only dinner."

"Can't you just admit it? You like the guy. A lot. And he obviously likes you. It's Christmas, Ivy. Nobody wants to be alone at Christmas."

They'd arrived at the square, which was anchored on the southern edge by the white-steepled United Methodist church. City workers were already busily setting up orange traffic cones in preparation for closing down the streets for the stroll.

"You can pull around the back and let me out there," Phoebe instructed, pointing at a narrow one-way lane that ran beside the church. Ivy followed her directions and parked in the church's lot, where a group of women were already gathering around a large, gaily painted wooden cart.

"You've still got an hour to kill before meeting up with Cody," Phoebe pointed out.

"Maybe I'll pop in and visit Lawrence Jones," Ivy said. "I think he'd get a kick out of seeing the Mrs. Santa dress again."

Phoebe lifted the lid of the cardboard box, revealing dozens of packages of individually wrapped and beautifully frosted and decorated Christmas cookies. "Here. Take him some of these, and tell him I said Merry Christmas."

The old man's eyes shone as he took in Ivy's splendid red velvet costume.

"Look at you," he said as she did a slow turn. "Is that Betty Rae Rose's costume you're wearing?"

"Possibly. I found it tucked away in the attic, but my friend Phoebe thinks it's maybe too small to have ever fit her."

"Betty Rae was a fine figure of a woman in her day," Mr. Jones said. "Just like you are now."

"Phoebe sent you some cookies from the Methodist church ladies auxiliary," Ivy said, offering him a packet of baked goods.

"How nice." He spread the cookies out on the coffee table, then looked back up at her. "I take it you changed your mind about going to the Christmas Stroll tonight?"

"I guess I did," Ivy said. "Somehow, I've managed to make three different commitments for tonight."

"You mean besides helping out Nancy Bergstrom?"

"Yes." She filled him in on Phoebe's predicament and her reluctant agreement to meet up with Cody and stall him until she was ready to meet her fiancé in person.

"You're kind of in a tight spot, aren't you?" He bit into a cookie and chewed, his brow wrinkled in thought. "Damned if you do and damned if you don't."

Ivy nodded her agreement. "I don't like lying to people. But I also don't want to disappoint Phoebe. She's been such a good friend to me, ever since I moved to Tarburton."

"Is there a way to meet this young man and let him know, without coming right out and saying it, that your friend hasn't been totally honest with him?"

"That's what I've been trying to figure out. I'm hoping I can find the right words, once I meet him face-to-face."

"And your third commitment for the evening? I hope you're going to dinner with your gentleman friend? The real estate agent?"

Ivy laughed. "You really missed your calling as a matchmaker, Lawrence. Yes, we have a date. I decided you're right. Time to move on and open myself up to new possibilities. Besides, how can I say no to a man who showed up at my door today with a new hot-water heater and a plumber to install it?"

"Good man," Lawrence said. "It sounds like you've got a jam-packed evening." His face took on a wistful expression. "I used to love going to the Christmas Stroll, getting out and seeing all the neighbors. And of course, the children, lining up to see Santa Claus."

"Why don't you come tonight?" Ivy said impulsively. "I've got to meet Cody in a few minutes, and then I promised to work for Nancy for an hour or so, but that still leaves me an hour until I meet up with my gentleman friend, as you call him. I could come back and pick you up."

"Oh no," he said quickly. "I'm really too old to be out at night like that. I'd only be a burden to you."

"I insist," Ivy said. "I mean, if you feel up to it."

"Well," he said slowly. "My doctor has been nagging me about getting out into the fresh air and doing more walking. He says it's good for my heart."

"That settles it. I'll pick you up a little before seven. Just make sure you dress warmly, okay?"

"I'll wear my heavy coat. And one of my great-niece's scarves. Which reminds me."

He pulled himself from his chair and retrieved a package from beneath the tabletop tree. It was wrapped in wrinkled green tissue paper that had obviously been recycled, and topped with a stick-on white bow. "A little Christmas gift, from me to you."

"Really?" Ivy blinked back sudden tears. She hadn't allowed herself to dwell on what a post-divorce Christmas morning would look like this year. True, under pressure, she'd given in and put up not one but two trees, but on this, her first Christmas by herself, she had no expectation of gifts. "But I don't have a gift for you, Lawrence."

"Your presence in my home is the best present of all," he said solemnly. "Now go on and open it."

She did as he instructed and ripped the paper from the package, revealing a whisper-soft pale pink scarf. "It's so beautiful," she said, stroking the fabric.

"It's real cashmere," he said excitedly. "I had my great-niece pick it out and overnight it to me. I'm not good with colors and things, but my late wife, she loved cashmere. She always said she'd rather have one or two nice things than a whole houseful of just okay."

Ivy wrapped the scarf around her neck. "I love it. And every time I wear it, I'll think of you."

He smiled. "I hope you will. But hadn't

you better run along to your meeting now?" He nodded in the direction of the ornate carved clock on his mantel. It was a quarter till five.

"You're right. But I'll be back here to pick you up by seven. Don't keep me waiting."

Ivy's pulse was racing as she rushed across the town square, ignoring the amused stares of passersby. She was running late because she'd had to circumnavigate all the side roads downtown, trying to find a parking space.

The clock in the tower was just beginning to chime five as she arrived, breathless, at the grouping of benches around the clock pavilion. A couple of teenage boys lounged on one bench, staring down at their cell phones, and an elderly woman, bundled up in layers of coats and scarves, sat opposite them, feeding pigeons from a small bag of potato chips.

Ivy's arrival caused a bit of the stir with the teenagers, who nudged and guffawed and pointed their cell phone cameras at her. Ivy nodded and acknowledged them with a finger wave.

Nearby, a gangly redheaded man paced back and forth, looking down at his own phone. He was younger than Ivy, mid- to late twenties, she thought, with the pale, freckled complexion that went with the ginger hair. He wore a puffy black down-filled jacket, the hem of which he kept trying, in vain, to tug downward. As she drew closer, Ivy spied the source of his agitation: a huge damp brown stain covered the front of his stiffly starched khaki pants.

Ivy could sense his discomfort from where she stood, several yards away, searching the vicinity for Phoebe's fiancé, Cody. People were hurrying by, headed in the direction of the booths being set up for the Christmas Stroll, but nobody else resembled the photos Phoebe had shown her of her Army Ranger stud muffin.

Ivy shrugged and leaned against one of the pavilion's concrete columns. It was only five after. Maybe Cody was still circling the square, trying to find a parking place. Maybe he'd been delayed by all the traffic choking the downtown streets. Or maybe, like Phoebe, he was experiencing cold feet. Ivy pulled her phone from the pocket of her skirt. No missed calls or texts from Phoebe.

After ten more minutes, Ivy's own feet were literally getting cold. The teenagers got up and moved on and the pigeon lady finished scattering chips for the birds, but the redhead continued pacing. Ivy moved over to the vacated bench, hunching her shoulders and wrapping the cashmere scarf tighter around her neck. She was studying her own phone, trying to decide if she should alert Phoebe that she'd been stood up, when she felt a slight tap on her shoulder.

It was the redhead. His cheeks were stained pink, either from the cold or with embarrassment. "Uh, ma'am? Excuse me. Hate to bother you, but I'm supposed to be meeting somebody here and she's fifteen minutes late and I'm starting to get worried about her. Maybe you know her? Phoebe Huddleston? Works at the courthouse?"

Ivy stared at the young man, who in no way resembled her friend's fiancé.

CHAPTER 20

"Are you . . . Cody?"

"Yeah. I'm Cody," he said eagerly. "So, do you know Phoebe? Is she okay? I'm getting kind of worried about her."

Ivy made a split-second decision.

"She's fine. It's kind of a long story." She patted the seat of the bench. "Why don't you sit down and I'll explain."

He perched on the edge of the bench. For the first time, Ivy noticed he was clutching something in his right hand. It was a single, sadly wilted daisy. He tugged self-consciously at the hem of his jacket again.

"What happened to you?" Ivy asked.

His cheeks blazed a deep red and he shook his head in disbelief. "You wouldn't believe it if I told you."

"Try me. My name is Ivy, by the way."

He ran long, pale fingers through the short red stubble of his hair. "Hi, Ivy. Nice to meet you. The reason I was late getting here was, I got T-boned by an elf."

Ivy struggled to maintain her composure. "Like, a real elf?"

"Okay, it was some hot chick dressed in an elf costume. She was pushing this sort of wagon thing across the square, not really looking where she was going, and I guess maybe I was concentrating on getting here on time . . . anyway, she basically ran right into me. There was a big vat of hot cocoa on the cart, and of course, it splashed all over my crotch. . . ." He pointed in the general vicinity.

"Now I look like a loser, and my girl when she gets here is gonna think I peed my pants. Talk about lousy first impressions."

"I see. Did this elf say anything, after she assaulted you with her cocoa cart?"

"It was technically a cookies and cocoa cart. For some church. I mean, she said she was sorry, like a dozen times, and she kept, like, trying to mop it up, which only made a bigger mess. And then, I guess she could tell I was pretty upset, so she gave me all these cookies. . . ."

He stuck his hand into his jacket pocket and brought out half a dozen wrapped Christmas cookies.

Ivy had to bite her lower lip to suppress the laughter beginning to bubble up from deep within her chest.

Cody noted her odd expression and for the first time seemed to notice how she was dressed.

"Hey. So, if you're Mrs. Santa Claus — is that elf, like, part of your posse or something?"

She chose her words carefully. "We know each other, if that's what you mean."

"And does this elf know Phoebe?"

Ivy could only nod.

"Huh. So anyway, have you talked to Phoebe today? I mean, she's coming, right?"

Ivy decided to cut to the chase. "So, Cody. Phoebe showed me the photos from your online profile, and I just have to point out, you don't look anything like those pictures. In fact, that's not you at all. Am I right?"

He hung his head and mumbled something.

"I'm sorry?"

Now he looked her directly in the eyes. "I'm an idiot, okay? You're right. Those pictures are fakes. Like me. Big, fat fakes. Which is why I came here today. I had to tell Phoebe the truth about me. No matter what. She deserves that."

"Is any of it true?" Ivy asked gently. "I mean, is your name really Cody? Did you actually just get out of the Army?"

"Hell yeah, that part is true," he said, looking offended. He reached for his wallet. "I'll show you my driver's license and military ID, if you don't believe me."

"Not necessary," Ivy said. "But why? If you're who you say you are, why the phony pictures?"

"Are you kidding? Look at me. I'm six-foot-six, weigh one hundred and sixty pounds. I've got this stinking red hair and freckles. I'm like a comic book freak. What girl would fall for somebody who looks like me?"

"Phoebe."

"No." He shook his head emphatically. "She fell in love with whoever that dude is. I checked it out. He's some catalog model. His name is Estefan. No last name. Some guys in my unit, they told me about this internet site, you can download photos for free." He ran his hands through his short-cropped hair again. "It was Saturday night; I was lonely; I hadn't had a real girlfriend since I left home for basic training. I thought, what the hell. Give it a shot. So I made a profile for myself, using the fake photos, and I just randomly started following cute girls I found on social media."

"That Estefan was some hottie. I bet you got lots of responses," Ivy said.

He rolled his eyes. "You don't want to know. What kind of girl sends nude selfies to a stranger?" His face was pinking up again. "There are some sicko chicks out there. But not Phoebe. I liked her right away. Yeah, she's beautiful, but she's so normal, you know? So real."

"Real." She left the word hanging there in the frigid air.

"Yeah. She told me how it took her, like, six years to finish college, because she was working and could only take a few classes at a time, because she works for the county. I liked that she's lived in the same town her whole life, and that she's close to her family. Me? My parents are divorced. They both remarried, and I'm not that crazy about being the stepkid. The more Phoebe and I wrote each other, the more we found out we have in common. She told me I'm the only guy she's ever known who actually likes cats."

Ivy smiled. That all sounded exactly like the Phoebe she'd come to know since moving to Tarburton.

"When she mentioned that she was a *Star Wars* freak, that did it. I knew she was the one. We'd have these long conversations while I was deployed. Like, for hours. I loved her voice, that soft southern accent, and the way she sort of hiccups a little when she laughs. And when she says my name? 'Co-deeeee.' The way it sort of pours out of her mouth, smooth and sweet, like honey. Nobody's ever said my name that way."

Cody jumped up from the bench and began pacing again. "I almost didn't come today. I was so scared about what Phoebe would say when she met the real me, driving over here today I had to pull off the road and puke in some bushes in some random person's yard."

"But you came anyway," Ivy observed. "That takes guts."

"I had to. I mean, we're getting married! At least, I hope we are. But probably, when she sees what I really look like, she'll turn around and run the other way."

He tugged at the hem of his jacket again and did a slow turn, his eyes searching the approaching darkness for a glimpse of his elusive fiancée. Then he was looking directly at Ivy, his face etched with a haunting sadness.

"I get it. She's not coming at all, right? That's why she sent you. To break up with me."

"No! That's not it at all." Ivy felt her phone buzzing in her pocket. She took it out and silently read the text message:

What did he say? Does he hate me?

Ivy jumped to her feet and grabbed Cody's hand. "Come with me."

He pulled away for a second. "Where are we going?"

"We're going to put an end to this comedy of errors. Once and for all."

The square was thronged with people. It was full dark now, but every tree and bush and telephone pole bristled with twinkling white lights. They passed a small bandstand where a crowd had gathered to listen to a red-robed youth choir singing "Jingle Bells."

"Excuse me," Ivy said purposefully, parting the crowd as she pulled Cody along behind, ignoring the stares of townspeople obviously amused at seeing Mrs. Santa dragging a young man through the town square. As they neared the soldier's memorial statue, she spotted the rows of colorful booths that had been set up by local businesses and civic groups. They passed Rotarians selling hot pretzels, and Boy Scouts peddling doughnuts.

They passed the candy shop booth, which was done up with a candy-striped awning, and she waved at a harried Nancy Bergstrom, who was working solo. She gave Ivy a pleading look. "Be right back!" Ivy called.

"Hurry!" Nancy responded.

Finally, Ivy spotted a large wooden cart manned by a pair of white-haired church ladies, assisted by a familiar-looking elf, who was doling out cups of cocoa as fast as she could.

"Oh no," Cody said, stopping abruptly. "Not her again." He tried to back away, but Ivy pulled him forward.

"Excuse me!" she called, nearly shouting to make herself heard above the din of the festival.

Phoebe looked up, and when she saw Ivy the color drained from her face. She whispered something to one of the church ladies and hurried over, the bells on the toes of her booties jingling merrily with each step.

The front of her tunic was spattered with cocoa and her red cap sat crookedly atop her hair. "What happened? Where's Cody?"

"Here," Ivy said, releasing her grip on Phoebe's suitor's elbow. She took Cody's hand and forcibly placed it between her friend's two hands.

"Right here. Cody, meet Phoebe. You two need to talk. And I need to go do my job."

Chapter 21

As Ivy made her way back to the candy shop booth she was forced to dodge through a winding line of people — parents, small children, toddlers, and babies in strollers, waiting patiently for their turn to meet Santa.

The festival organizers had created a small village within the square, marked off with signs proclaiming it SANTALAND. There were gingerbread man cutouts and costumed elves directing parents through the lit maze leading toward an elevated platform. When she stood on her tiptoes she was able to make out the great man himself, seated on an ornately decorated gold throne, and even from where she stood, a hundred yards away, she could definitely hear the screaming protests of the toddler seated on his lap.

When she reached her destination, Nancy Bergstrom greeted her with a grateful hug.

"The Santa dress is perfect," Nancy said. "Wait. Was that Betty Rae's costume?"

"We think so. I found it up in an attic. Now, what do you need me to do?"

Nancy handed her a candy-striped apron and an iPad. "You can ring up the credit purchases. I'll help folks pick out their purchase and take care of the cash. Okay?"

She showed her new assistant her pricing and purchasing system and how to swipe credit cards through the square plugged into the iPad's USB port. "Just sing out if you have any problems."

Ivy spent the next hour ringing up and bagging what seemed like hundreds of boxes of Langley candies and fudge. As soon as she thought the rush of customers was slowing down, another wave would descend on the booth. But everyone seemed more than willing to wait their turn. People were patient, even jolly, complimenting her outfit and accepting samples of candy. More than one customer wanted to know if she was the "new Mrs. Claus," and every time she looked up, someone was asking to take her photo.

It was nearly seven o'clock before there was a brief lull in business. "Whew," Ivy said, turning to Nancy. "Is it always this intense?"

"We're usually pretty busy during the Christmas Stroll, but it's never been this crazy," Nancy said, beaming. "Part of it's probably the weather. Thank God we've got clear skies tonight. But I think mostly it's that Mrs. Santa costume of yours is a great draw." She reached out her hand for the iPad. "I want to run a quick total to see just how much we've sold."

She tapped some buttons on the tablet, and when the figure flashed on the screen her eyes widened. "Holy peppermint twist!" She held up the iPad for Ivy to see. "This is amazing. We've done more sales in the past hour than I've done all month in the shop. And December is always my best month."

"Yay!" Ivy said. She hesitated. "Nancy, it seems like it's slowed down a little. Would you hate me if I clock out? I promised Lawrence Jones I would pick him up and bring him to the stroll."

"You go on ahead," Nancy said. She pointed at the diminished stacks of pink-and-white-striped candy boxes on the booth's shelves. "I'm almost out of inventory anyway. Looks like we might even sell out pretty soon." She gave Ivy another hug. "Make sure you bring Lawrence over to see me. I want to thank him in person for connecting us."

■ ■ ■ ■

Lawrence was standing on the porch of his cottage, bundled up in a heavy woolen coat with a knit red-and-green scarf wrapped around his neck, when Ivy pulled into the driveway. "I'm sorry if I kept you waiting," she said, helping him into the passenger seat and stowing his walker in the back.

"Not at all," he said. His blue eyes shone with excitement. "I've been waving at my neighbors and enjoying seeing the beautiful lights on all the houses."

"The square is pretty crowded tonight," she warned. "I've never seen so many people out and about in this little town."

"It's not just folks from Tarburton, you know. People come from all over these mountains for the Christmas Stroll," he said, his head swiveling back and forth as he admired the downtown shops and streets lit up for the event.

She'd made one trip around the square and was beginning to despair of finding a parking slot when she spotted the taillights of a minivan backing out of a space on Main Street and quickly steered into the vacated spot.

"Are you ready?" she turned to ask her

passenger, but he'd already opened the door and was slowly pulling himself out of the vehicle.

"I think I can do without the walker tonight," he confided.

Ivy tucked the old man's hand in the crook of her arm as they made their way onto the square. "Lawrence, hello!" a stocky older man exclaimed, stopping to shake hands. "I haven't seen you out and about in quite a while. And who is your beautiful companion?"

"Gordon, this is my friend Ivy. She's new to town. Just bought Bob and Betty Rae Rose's old place. Ivy, this is Gordon Steinmetz. We used to be in Rotary together."

"Nice to meet you, Ivy," Steinmetz said, looking her up and down. "We're glad you're here. It's so great to see Four Roses all lit up again this year. And it looks like you're keeping up with all the Roses' traditions."

"Well, not all of them," Ivy said.

"I saw we've got our old Santa Claus back tonight too," Steinmetz said. "Is that your husband?"

Ivy felt herself blush. "Uh, no. That's actually my real estate agent. I offered to let him borrow the Santa suit for tonight."

"So you're a single gal? Aren't you afraid, living all alone in that broken-down old farmhouse way out in the country like that?"

"I'm in the process of renovating it," she said, her feelings a little hurt at this stranger's characterization of her farmhouse. "And it's not really broken down. It just needs a little love."

"Maybe Santa will bring you some power tools," Steinmetz said. "And a husband to use them."

Before she could reply, Lawrence was tugging on her arm. "Ivy, didn't you promise me some hot cocoa?"

Gordon Steinmetz wished them a Merry Christmas and walked away.

"Don't mind that old poop," Lawrence said, squeezing her arm. "Seems to me you're doing just fine on your own. I admire your spunk, moving here without knowing a soul, fixing up the farmhouse, and making new friends right away. What do you need with a husband?"

"I've already had a husband," Ivy agreed. "And he couldn't even change a lightbulb, let alone caulk a window. Besides, anything I need to learn how to do I can figure out from watching a YouTube tutorial."

"That's the spirit," Lawrence said.

■ ■ ■ ■

Several other people stopped the couple as they made their way across the square. Ivy met the neighbor who helped Lawrence with grocery shopping, and his pastor's wife, and a petite white-haired woman named Cora, who, Lawrence confided "is a widow lady who likes to drop by with casseroles."

"Your lady friend?" Ivy asked, her tone teasing.

"Well . . . she's a lady, and she's friendly," he said, thinking it over. "But I try not to encourage her because she's way too young for me, don't you think?"

"Age is a state of mind," Ivy replied. "But just how old is she?"

He gave it some thought. "I believe she's pushing eighty. But she still drives, and she owns her own home."

Ivy laughed and gave him a gentle nudge in the ribs. "Then I say go for it."

Ivy and Lawrence strolled slowly in the direction of the Methodist Church booth, stopping to linger and listen to a barbershop quartet's version of "White Christmas" at the bandstand. The old man tapped his foot in time to the four-part harmony, nodding his appreciation.

"Ever do any singing?" he asked Ivy.

"Only in the shower," she said. "I'm afraid I have a tin ear."

"My wife had a beautiful voice, and she played the piano too. Everett took after her," he said wistfully. "He sang baritone in the church choir. Had what they called perfect pitch. What I wouldn't give to hear them singing together right now."

Ivy detected a tremble in the old man's voice, and she squeezed his arm again. "Who knows? Maybe they're up in heaven right now, singing "Silent Night.""

"Maybe so," he said, his face brightening.

By the time they arrived at their destination, only a handful of customers stood around, sipping cocoa. The stand was manned by the same two women who'd been working earlier. One was busily counting the cash from a cigar box while the other bagged cookies for a customer.

Ivy paid for two cups of cocoa. "Excuse me, but what happened to Phoebe Huddleston?"

The church ladies exchanged a knowing look. "Oh, she and that young man wandered away quite a while ago," one of the women said, winking. "But we promised not to tattle to her grandmother that she left early. You're her friend Ivy, right?"

"Yes."

"She told us to tell you everything worked out just fine. And thanks."

Despite the cold, Ivy felt the same warm feeling settling over her body, and she was pretty sure it had nothing to do with the cocoa.

"Seems like you managed to help your friend after all," Lawrence observed. He clutched her arm a little tighter. "Say, do you think we could find a place to sit for a spell? These old legs of mine are suddenly feeling pretty weak."

"Of course," Ivy said. She took out her cell phone to check the time. It was five after eight. And she had a text message from Ezra:

Come early, okay? There's someone who wants to meet you.

"Lawrence, would it be all right if we dropped by Santaland? There's somebody there who my real estate agent wants me to meet. When I was by there earlier I noticed that there are lots of benches, and you can rest a little bit before I take you home."

"Whatever you say, Ivy. I hate to be a burden, especially when you've got a big night planned with your young man."

"You aren't a burden, Lawrence. You're an absolute bright spot in my life." She deftly typed a response to Ezra's earlier message:

On my way.

Ivy steered them in the direction of Santaland. The crowd in the square seemed to have thinned out substantially, and when they entered the gingerbread entrance to the village only two children and their mother were still waiting in line. As Ivy and Lawrence approached, a costumed teenage elf approached.

"Hey, uh, sorry, but Santa's only here for another ten minutes, so nobody else can get in line now. He's, uh, gotta get back to the North Pole, you know?"

"I'm actually a friend of Santa's," Ivy told the kid. "We're just going to sit on one of the benches and wait for him to get off shift."

The kid shrugged. "Cool. I guess."

They found a bench at the edge of the platform and sat down. A pair of towheaded children, a boy and his sister who looked to be about five or six, were inching toward the throne, glancing backward at their mother, who seemed to be coaching them from the sidelines.

"Come right up, children," Santa boomed.

"Have you been good this year?"

The little girl stuck her thumb in her mouth and backed away, but her younger brother hopped right onto Santa's lap. Ezra glanced over and smiled broadly when he saw Ivy and her companion. He gave them a quick thumbs-up and mouthed, *Five minutes.*

"He makes a pretty convincing Santa," Lawrence observed. "Of course, he's not as plump as Santa Bob was, but the children don't seem to mind."

Ezra was leaning forward, patiently attempting to coax the timid little girl to approach. Ivy leaned forward to listen.

"Hi there," he said. "What's your name?"

The child whispered something inaudible. Ezra held his hand to his ear. "I didn't quite hear that. Did you say your name is Snowflake?"

The little girl giggled and shook her head.

"Is it Rainbow?"

She shook her head again and took a step forward.

"I know. It's Moonbeam. Right? You definitely look like a Moonbeam to me."

"No!" the little girl said, her hands on her hips. "My name is Violet, you silly Santa."

Ezra chuckled. "Well, Violet, I have to head for the North Pole pretty soon. Your brother already told me about the LEGO set he wants, so would you like to tell me what's on your Christmas list?"

"Violet!" Her mother's voice was sharp. "Daddy's waiting in the car. And Santa is a very busy man."

The little girl took two steps. She leaned in and tugged at Ezra's fake beard. "I want a pony and a puppy and a real live unicorn!" she yelled.

Violet's mother shook her head vigorously, giving Santa the cutoff signal.

"This probably isn't the year for a pony or a puppy," he said apologetically. "And real unicorns are almost impossible to catch, but I'm sure you'll find something you'll love under the tree on Christmas morning."

"Thanks, Santa," the mother said. She clambered onto the platform and took each child by the hand, dragging them away as the little girl tearfully protested that she really, really wanted a unicorn.

When the family was out of view Ezra stood up and climbed down from the platform. He looked around to make sure there were no children in view, then removed the fake beard and tucked it in the pocket of his jacket.

Ivy stood up to meet him, and his eyes widened as he took in her costume. "Wow," he said, grasping her hands. "You look amazing. Where did this come from?"

"I found it in the attic yesterday, when I went looking for a tree stand."

"It looks like it was made for you." He leaned in and kissed her lightly. "Did I already tell you how beautiful you look in it?"

Ivy felt herself blushing. Her companion tactfully cleared his throat.

She whirled around and touched him on the shoulder. "How rude of me. I want you to meet my friend Lawrence."

Ezra stuck out his hand. "Hi, Lawrence. Nice to meet you."

The old man shook his hand. "We were watching you with those children up there. You made an outstanding Santa Claus. I'm sure Bob Rose would be proud of your performance."

"I'm back!" A middle-aged woman walked rapidly toward them from behind the raised platform. She wore a stylish calf-length coat, high-heeled boots, and a fur hat that obscured her hair.

"There you are," Ezra said. "I wondered where you'd gotten off to."

"I was just talking to the city maintenance people about breaking down your platform and moving the throne back into storage," the woman answered. "And I wanted to make sure those kids who worked as elves all got paid. Now we're all set."

"Mom, I want you to meet Ivy Perkins," Ezra said.

Ivy looked from Ezra to his mother. "Mom? I thought you said I was meeting your broker."

"He hates telling people his broker is his mother," the woman said, laughing. She took both of Ivy's hands in hers. "I'm Carlette Wheeler. And I've been dying to meet you, Ivy."

Chapter 22

Lawrence Jones struggled to his feet. "Did you say your name is Carlette?" His voice cracked with emotion.

Ivy felt a tingle travel down her spine.

"That's right."

Lawrence seemed to sway slightly on his feet and she reached out an arm to steady the older man.

"Are you . . . are you from around here?" he croaked.

Carlette Wheeler seemed taken aback by the question. "My father's people were from Tarburton. But after he was killed in action in Vietnam, my mother and I moved away. She remarried a couple years later. I only moved back to the area recently, after Ezra convinced me to open a brokerage in Asheville."

The old man blinked rapidly. "Your son's name is Ezra?" He coughed and his grip tightened on Ivy's arm. "You don't hear that name very often these days."

"Tell me about it," Ezra said. "I was always the only Ezra in my class."

"I didn't want you to be just another Jason or Jeremy or Justin," Carlette said. "So I named you —"

"After your father's father," Lawrence said softly.

Carlette Wheeler stared at the old man. "How could you know that?"

Ivy felt his hand trembling beneath her own. "Your father's name was Everett Jones. He was an Eagle Scout. He sang baritone and he played shortstop in high school. And he had red hair. Just like yours."

Carlette's hand flew to her head. She removed the hat and shook her hair loose. The auburn mane was shot through with silver. "I don't understand."

Lawrence Jones staggered as his legs seemed to collapse beneath him. Ezra caught him before he hit the ground, easily transferring him to the bench, where he sat beside him. "Are you all right?" He looked up at Ivy. "Should we call an ambulance or something?"

"No," Lawrence said. He clutched Ezra's arm, searching his face. "I'm not having a heart attack. I'm having . . ." He shook his head numbly and nodded at Ivy.

"I think Lawrence is probably in shock," she told Carlette. "How old are you?"

"Me? I'm fifty-seven. Why?"

"Let me ask you another question," Ivy said. "Do you remember going to see Santa Claus? Right here in Tarburton, when you were a little girl?"

Carlette hesitated and then nodded, looking off across the square with a faraway expression. "Mama and I moved here while Daddy was in Vietnam. I think we were only here for a year or two. We lived in my grandparents' house, because Granddaddy's job transferred him somewhere on the West Coast. I remember that Christmas, Mama was so sad all the time. I didn't know it at the time, but she'd gotten word that Daddy was missing in action. Anyway, I can remember I had a beautiful dress, red plaid, I think, that my grandmother had made for me. Mama took me to this department store to see their Santa Claus. Ezra tells me the store's been closed for years."

"Atkins," Lawrence said.

"Do you remember handing a note to Santa?" Ivy asked.

"Mama had me write notes to Santa every year. I kept it up until I was a teenager, sort of as a joke, I guess. When she died, I was going through her things and I found a bunch of them, in an old cigar box. She kept all my notes to Santa."

"Except that one?" Ivy asked.

"When she told me we were going to see Santa, I insisted on handing him the letter myself. I wouldn't even let Mama read it because it was going to be a secret, between me and Santa Claus, so Mama would be surprised, Christmas morning, when she woke up and Daddy was back home."

"Oh God," Ezra murmured.

"I think that's probably the year I stopped believing," Carlette said. "I had to keep pretending, for Mama's sake, but that was the year I knew." She looked across the square, at the bronze statue of the soldier, standing sentry in the night. "It's been a long time since I let myself believe in anything, if you want to know the truth."

"We were holding out hope that he'd be found alive," Lawrence said sadly. "We didn't want to spoil your Christmas."

Carlette raised an eyebrow. "We?"

"Your grandmother and I. And your mother, of course," Lawrence said. He fumbled in the pocket of his coat, but when he came up empty-handed Ivy gave him the delicate Christmas hanky she'd tucked into her own pocket. He dabbed his eyes with the hanky, then reached out his hand and took Carlette's in his.

"Everett was our only child. He was everything to us. You were everything to us, Carlette."

Chapter 23

Carlette Wheeler sank down onto the bench beside the old man. Her eyes filled with tears and her hands trembled as she moved to wipe them away. "I don't know what to say. How can this be? It's been so many years. I always just assumed . . ."

"I was dead?" Lawrence managed a feeble laugh.

"So . . . how old are you?"

"I'm ninety-six."

"And Granny?"

"She's been gone a long time now. Passed away while we were living out west. And your mother, Diana? Is she still . . ."

"No. She died when Ezra was in kindergarten."

Ezra looked up at Ivy. "How did you know?"

"I didn't," Ivy said. "I had no clue." She touched his shoulder. "It started with this Santa suit. Remember? That first night I moved into the farmhouse, we found this outfit in a box on the closet shelf."

"Right. But what's that got to do with anything?"

"After you left, I was putting the Santa suit away and I found a piece of paper in the pocket. It was a letter from a little girl."

"A letter to Santa Claus," Lawrence said.

"From a little girl named Carlette," Ivy finished. "I kept wondering how that story ended. Okay, maybe I was slightly obsessed. I'd become friends with a woman who works at the courthouse: Phoebe. I showed her the letter, and she knew immediately who'd written it, because her mother grew up across the street from that house where you were living and she talked a lot about her best friend, Carlette."

"Sally? Are you talking about Sally Finley? She still lives here?" Carlette asked.

"Her name is Huddleston now, but yes, she still lives in town," Ivy said. "She told me the address of her childhood home and described the house across the street where you lived back then. I don't know what came over me, but one day I just knocked on the door and introduced myself to the man who was living there."

Carlette's eyes had a faraway look. "I remember the house on Spruce Street.

There was a chinaberry tree in the front yard. With a tire swing. And a one-car garage Sally and I called our clubhouse."

"The tire swing is gone, but the chinaberry tree is still there," Lawrence said. "Like me."

"All these years," Carlette said wonderingly. "You were right here, Granddaddy, but I had no idea. After Daddy died, I think Mama just wanted to put Tarburton in the past. It was too sad for her. My stepdad, Walter, was a good man. He adopted me when I was ten, and Mama never wanted to look back. Walter was in sales, so we moved around a good bit, and somehow, I lost track."

"You sent me a postcard from Disney World. I still have it. Along with your high school graduation announcement," Lawrence said.

"I remember you always sent me birthday and Christmas cards — always with puppies on them, and always with a ten-dollar bill tucked inside," Carlette said. She made a wry face. "And I probably never wrote back to say thank you. I was such a brat."

"You were just a kid," Lawrence said. "I never held it against Diana for remarrying after Ev died. She was too young to stay a widow. Especially with a kid to raise on her own. But I always hoped somehow I'd see you again someday. And now, here you are. And with a son of your own. My great-grandson!" He shook his head. "It's almost too much for me to take in."

Carlette looked up at Ivy, who was already feeling like an awkward third wheel in this unlikely and unfolding family reunion. "And it's all because of you."

"It wasn't me," Ivy insisted. "It was the Santa suit. And Ezra. If he hadn't insisted on helping me get settled in the farmhouse, hadn't been such a *nuisance* about showing up to replace windows and get the furnace working, and move out the Roses' old furniture and then turn around and move it back in again — I never would have found your note in the jacket pocket."

"Nobody else would have gone out of their way to figure out what happened to that little girl and her MIA father," Ezra said. "Nobody else would have been brave enough to buy an old farmhouse, sight unseen, and move to a town where she didn't know a soul. . . ."

"Nobody else would have befriended a lonely old geezer like me," Lawrence said.

"Ivy!"

The bells on the tips of the grown-up elf's booties jingled as she dashed toward the group assembled in Santaland, dragging along a very tall redheaded young man.

"Cody and I have been looking all over for you!" Phoebe exclaimed, throwing her arms around her friend. "We were afraid you'd already left for dinner. You'll never guess —"

Noticing the two strangers sitting on the bench, she stopped short. "Oh. Sorry. Am I interrupting something?"

"Phoebe, you already know Ezra. But I'd like you to meet Lawrence Jones. And this is Ezra's mom — and Lawrence's granddaughter — Carlette Wheeler."

"What? That Carlette? The girl from the Santa note? No way!" Phoebe blurted, then covered her mouth with her hands. "That's amazing. I can't believe you actually found her."

"It wasn't me," Ivy said. "It was the Santa suit." She gave her friend an appraising glance. Phoebe's face was aglow with happiness, and she noticed that Cody was grinning too.

"So? What's the big news? Don't tell me you moved up the wedding date."

"Nope. We moved it back. You were right. It turns out we still have a lot to learn about each other."

"We're absolutely still getting married,"

Cody put in, slinging an arm around his girl's shoulder. "She's promised me she won't back out. Even though I'm not that buff guy from the fake online profile."

"You're a thousand times better than that dude," Phoebe said, gazing up at him with puppy eyes. "A million times better. Better than Han Solo even."

Cody tightened his hold on her. "And you're so much more beautiful, more real, more fun, than I could have ever hoped for. You're my Princess Leia."

"We're headed over to my mom's house right now, so she can meet him," Phoebe said. "You were right about that too, Ivy. It would break her heart if I just snuck off and eloped with a stranger. Anyway, I know she'll fall in love with Cody, just like I did."

"So when's the wedding?" Ivy asked.

"It can't be too soon for me," Cody said.

"We're going to slow things down a little bit," Phoebe said. "Now that he's home, I want us to go on real dates and have a real romance."

"But not too many dates," Cody said, locking eyes with her. "Just in case she changes her mind."

"I won't," Phoebe promised. "Ever."

Ivy felt something cold and wet land on her cheek. She looked up at the sky and pointed. "Hey, look. It's starting to snow."

It was true. The cobalt sky was streaked with snowflakes and it was coming down fast, frosting her red velvet dress, the winter-dried grass, and the glossy green leaves of the magnolia trees in the square.

She held out her hand and watched a flake land on her fingertip. "Maybe we'll have a white Christmas."

Phoebe tugged at Cody's hand. "We'd better get going. My mom's house is at the top of a steep hill, and if it starts to ice over we'll never make it."

Lawrence Jones's head lolled against the back of the park bench. His eyes were closed and he was softly snoring.

"He's asleep," Ivy said, smiling. She looked up at Ezra. "This was a lot of excitement for him tonight. I'd better get Lawrence home. Can we postpone dinner?"

"Don't you dare," Carlette said. "I'm happy to take him home." She gently shook the old man's shoulder. "Granddad?"

The old man's eyes fluttered, then opened. "Sorry. Guess I must have dozed off. I'm not really used to being out and about this late at night."

"Mom and I are going to walk you to her car, and she's going to give you a ride home," Ezra said. He offered Lawrence his arm and eased him to his feet.

"Would you look at that?" Lawrence exclaimed, holding out the sleeve of his coat, which had already accumulated a dusting of flakes. "It's snowing!"

Chapter 24

By the time they met up again at the soldier's memorial statue, half an inch of snow had accumulated on the park benches, the ground, and even the bronze soldier himself. Ivy was grateful for the cashmere scarf Lawrence had gifted her and for the wool tights under the Mrs. Santa dress, but she was shivering, rubbing her arms in a vain attempt to keep warm.

"You need a coat!" Ezra exclaimed as he walked up, his boots crunching on the frosty sidewalk.

"What about you?" Ivy retorted.

"I'm wearing thermal long johns and two pairs of socks. Mom's idea," he admitted. "Come on, let's head over to the restaurant. You're freezing and I'm starved."

"This snow is coming down pretty fast," Ivy pointed out. "You know, I've been living in Atlanta so long, I haven't really driven in this kind of weather in a long time. Maybe

we really should rethink the restaurant."
Ezra's face fell. "I thought we had a deal. Dinner in exchange for plumbing services."
"How about dinner at my place?"
"You cook?"
"Oh yes," she said airily. "I can cook anything you like, but the house specialty is the happy waitress."
"Huh?"
"You've never had a happy waitress?"
"That's a food option?"
"You'll love it," Ivy promised.

She removed the ice tray from the freezer, cracked some cubes into a jelly jar, then poured an inch of bourbon over the cubes and handed it to Ezra, who was seated at the kitchen table with Punkin hovering close by.
The Santa suit jacket hung on the back of Ezra's chair and he'd removed the boots, but only after he'd gone out to the henhouse to check on Ivy's chickens.
"They're snug in their roosts." He looked around the kitchen, then back at Ivy, standing at the old-fashioned stove, melting butter in a black cast-iron skillet. She'd tied one of Betty Rae's aprons over her velvet dress and was sipping a glass of wine. "Like you."

She turned and smiled. "You know, when I saw this kitchen in the online listing I thought the first thing I'd do would be to rip out everything in here. Get some granite countertops and stainless-steel appliances . . ."

"And now?"

"Well, I wouldn't mind having a real ice maker, and some drawers that didn't stick, but otherwise, I've kind of gotten used to the place."

"It suits you," Ezra said.

She plopped a piece of bread into the skillet, laid a slab of cheddar cheese on top of that, added a tomato slice and topped it with two pieces of cooked bacon. When she was satisfied that the bread was grilled and the cheese was melted, she slid the open-faced sandwich onto one of Betty Rae's Christmas plates. She added a pickle spear and a handful of potato chips, then presented the dish to her guest.

"Et voilà! One happy waitress."

"Where's yours?"

"I'm not all that hungry," Ivy said, leaning over and helping herself to one of his chips.

Ezra caught her by the waist and deftly lifted her onto his lap. "I'm happy to share mine," he said. He took a bite of the sandwich, chewed, and rolled his eyes dramatically.

"Best sandwich ever. Where'd you learn to make this?"

"My friend Meg. She's a Jersey girl and she turned me on to the happy waitress. It's what you order at a diner after a night of partying."

"Like Waffle House, only different," Ezra said. He demolished the sandwich and the chips in a matter of minutes, then pushed the plate away.

"Still disappointed about not going out to dinner?" Ivy asked, wrapping her arms around his neck.

His kiss was his answer.

"This is much, much better," he said finally. He looked over her shoulder, out the kitchen window, where the snow was falling at a furious rate. "Wow. It's really coming down now."

Ivy stood up and went to the kitchen door to see for herself. The ground outside was completely blanketed. She shivered. "I hope the girls will be okay."

Ezra stood in back of her. "They'll be fine. I turned on the space heater for them. Those have got to be the most spoiled chickens in North Carolina." He nuzzled the back of her neck with his chin. "You smell nice. Like . . . um . . . flowers. And snow." He lifted his nose and sniffed. "Something else too. Maybe . . . peppermint?"

"Well, I was selling candy for Nancy Bergstrom earlier tonight," Ivy said, laughing. "I guess that's not a bad way to smell, right?"

"Delicious." Ezra kissed her neck. He slowly turned her to face him. "Delicious dinner. Delicious you." His fingers searched in vain for the hidden buttons on the front of the snug-fitting velvet jacket. He frowned. "Is this some kind of a trick?"

Ivy kissed him, moving her lips against his. "Shall I show you?"

"Either that, or I rip this friggin' thing off over your head," Ezra muttered, slipping his hands beneath the jacket.

"Let's not do that." Ivy giggled. "Think how disappointed the children of Tarburton would be if Mrs. Santa's dress was ruined."

"Not as disappointed as me, unless I get you naked, very, very soon," Ezra said, tugging at the stubborn metal zipper on the skirt.

"Follow me," Ivy said. She took his hand and led him toward the bedroom.

Chapter 25

At some point later in the evening, Ivy and Ezra made their way to the living room, where they sprawled on the sofa in front of the fireplace, tangled up in arms and legs and a jumble of hastily discarded clothing. Again. The room was dark except for the glowing multicolored lights of the Christmas tree and the crackling fire. Punkin snored softly from his bed in the corner.

Ivy rested her head on Ezra's chest and shivered slightly, prompting him to cover her bare back with the velvet jacket of the Santa suit.

"Wonder what the Roses would say about all of this?" Ivy said.

Ezra yawned and lazily ran a fingertip down her bare spine. "I think they'd approve. You've brought this old place to life. You know, I loved this farmhouse the minute I saw it. The place was crying out to be lived in again. But when I listed it, my expectations for a sale were pretty low. I even told James he'd never get his asking price."

"And he didn't," Ivy pointed out.

"You were a damned tough negotiator," Ezra said, laughing.

"What you didn't know was that buying this place totally maxed me out. My savings, my IRAs, my half of the equity in our house after the divorce, everything I had. It was a huge leap of faith."

Ivy stopped herself. "Faith isn't something I've had a lot of, over the years. I think I stopped believing good things would happen the year I asked a sketchy-looking mall Santa to bring my mother home for Christmas. I was about the same age as your mom when she stopped believing."

"I'm guessing she didn't come home?" Ezra asked gently.

"No. She had pancreatic cancer. It was . . . fast. And brutal," Ivy said. She shrugged. "Anyway, when I made the offer on this house, I was afraid the seller wouldn't accept my offer and terrified he would."

"We actually had a way better offer on the table," Ezra said.

"Huh?" Ivy sat upright, wrapping the jacket around herself.

"I wasn't supposed to tell you. That real

estate developer I told you about, the one who bought the abandoned textile mill? He made us a pretty respectable offer for Four Roses Farm. Like, one hundred and fifty thousand dollars more."

"And James didn't accept? Why on earth not?"

"The guy wanted to tear down the farmhouse and build a town-home subdivision. James Heywood said his father-in-law would have turned over in his grave. He wanted the house to go to a special buyer."

"What's so special about me?"

Ezra kissed her shoulder. "If I tell you, will you promise not to report me to the real estate ethics police?"

"Hmmm. I don't know. This sounds serious."

"Okay, here goes. I kinda cyberstalked you."

She feigned outrage. "You what?"

"I had my client's fiduciary interest to protect. And yeah, I was more than curious to find out about this mysterious I. G. Perkins. So I looked you up on Facebook and Instagram and LinkedIn. You're not much of a poster, are you?"

Ivy stared into the flames. "When Kyle and I split up, I couldn't bear to see all those happy photos of us snorkeling in Cancún, or hiking in the mountains — or the two of us at dinner with Bianca, my BFF-slash-client who it turns out he was sleeping with on the side. It all seemed like such a lie, so I deleted everything. Clean slate, right?"

"There's no such thing as going quiet on the internet, though," Ezra reminded her. "I found mentions of you in the Atlanta paper when you landed a big client — and when you left the company you'd helped start."

"Yeah, 'left' is PR spin for 'forced out,' " Ivy said, looking up at him.

"I, uh, also stalked your ex. I even saw the wedding photos of him and Restaurant Barbie."

Ivy's voice sounded a warning note. "Getting kinda creepy here, dude."

"No worries. I unfollowed. He's not even very interesting."

"You still haven't told me why James decided to accept my lowball offer," she pointed out.

"It was James's idea. He wanted to know all about the woman who was buying Four Roses Farm. So I followed your digital footprint. Found your name on the website you volunteered to design for that animal rescue nonprofit in Atlanta."

Ivy yawned and pushed an errant strand

of hair out of her eye. "Lots of people do volunteer work."

"Not as many as you'd think. After I listed the farmhouse, I started talking to the locals about Bob and Betty Rae Rose. They were pretty remarkable folks. They were Jewish — did you know that?"

"I found a little mezuzah nailed above the front door, so I did wonder about that," Ivy said. "It made the whole Christmas connection pretty intriguing."

"That community thrift store you donated all this furniture to — before buying it back? Betty Rae started that, as a fundraiser for a shelter for battered women. Bob donated the money to build the shelter. He also financed the obstetrics wing for the hospital, and started a college scholarship fund for deserving seniors graduating from the local high school. And he did it all anonymously; in fact, he insisted that his donations be kept a secret."

"Then how did you find out about all his good works?" Ivy asked.

"I've become pretty good friends with the loan officer at the local bank," Ezra said. "We were having lunch and I mentioned I'd tracked down the owner of Four Roses Farm, and he let it slip that Bob and Betty Rae had been longtime benefactors to the community."

"Oh my gosh!" Ivy exclaimed. She told Ezra about the scribbled notations on the Santa Claus letters she'd found in the old trunk that was now serving as the cottage's living room coffee table.

"The letters with the notes — they were all from kids who seemed to be pretty needy," she said slowly. "I bet Bob Rose made it his business to make sure those kids got what they'd asked for on Christmas morning — an Easy-Bake Oven for a little girl whose mother's stove was broken, a catcher's mitt for a kid whose father was out of work. . . ."

"And then there was the little girl named Carlette who just wanted her daddy to come home from the war," Ezra said quietly. "The one wish it was out of Bob Rose's power to grant."

"Yeah." Ivy sighed. "I bet that's why he kept that note in the pocket of the Santa suit. As a reminder."

"Or maybe he left it there, all those years ago, in the hopes that someone like you would find that note and figure out what happened to Carlette's father." Ezra raised his head and put a finger under Ivy's chin. "You know what all you did today, right? You helped my mom connect with her grandfather — her only living relative other than me. You introduced me to my great-grandfather — the one I'm named after. Yeah — while we were walking him to my mom's car he told me the *E* in 'Lawrence E. Jones' stands for 'Ezra.' You played Cupid for your friend Phoebe and her guy, Cody. And let's not forget — you seem to have single-handedly saved Langley Sweets. You must be exhausted, Ivy Perkins."

"I keep trying to tell you, it wasn't me," Ivy insisted. She pulled the velvet jacket tighter around her shoulders. "It was the power of the Santa suit. I was just the person who happened to be in the right place at the right time."

She gazed around at the darkened living room, at the homely but well-loved furnishings, the glowing, slightly tilting Christmas tree, and out the front windows, where the twinkling white fairy lights were reflected in the still-falling snow.

"The minute I saw those online photographs of the Four Roses farmhouse, I knew I would buy it," she said. "I knew I'd found my home."

"No," Ezra said, shaking his head. "I think it was the other way around. I think this old place found you. This farmhouse was just standing here, waiting. James told me he'd had other agents wanting to list the place in the past, but the time was never right. And then, suddenly, the time was right. I saw a photo of you, with Punkin, when he was a puppy, and I looked at you and knew the two of you needed to own this old house. When I told James what I found out about his buyer, a woman named Ivy Perkins, he said okay immediately. Because he was waiting, as Bob and Betty Rae would have wanted, to make sure that Four Roses Farm was ending up in the right hands."

Ezra kissed Ivy's right and then left palm. "Your hands."

Then he clasped both her hands between his. "Our hands?"

Punkin roused himself from his nearby nest and sleepily climbed onto the sofa, wedging himself between Ivy's and Ezra's intertwined bodies. He licked Ezra's chin.

Ivy nodded. "Ours."

ACKNOWLEDGMENTS

Dear Readers: Please consider *The Santa Suit* my holiday gift to you after a life-altering year like 2021. Your support and encouragement have meant everything to me every year over the past three decades, but never more than this past year.

I never intended to write a *second* book in the year of the pandemic, and in fact, I kept this project a secret until it was almost completely written. But on a long, boring drive to Tybee Island last fall, I had the spark of an idea. My writer pals from *Friends & Fiction:* Kristin Harmel, Kristy Woodson Harvey, Patti Callahan Henry, and Mary Alice Monroe were kind enough to listen and add their encouragement. Mostly, this Christmas novella was written in bed, during 7 a.m. writing sprints, with my pals cheering me on through lengthy text chains, and my husband, Tom, keeping me alternately supplied with mugs of Earl

Grey tea and iced Diet Coke. I'm so grateful to him, our family, and of course, my longtime publishing team: Stuart Krichevsky of the Stuart Krichevsky Literary Agency, my editor/publisher, Jen Enderlin, and the entire team at St. Martin's Press, especially the indispensable publicity/marketing duo I have nicknamed Jerica — Jessica Zimmerman and Erica Martirano.

Huge thanks also to Michael Storrings for another adorable cover, and of course, I owe a huge debt to my indispensable marketing guru, confidante, and stalwart book tour roadie, Meghan Walker of Tandem Literary.

ABOUT THE AUTHOR

Mary Kay Andrews is The *New York Times* bestselling author of *Hello, Summer, Sunset Beach, The High Tide Club, The Beach House Cookbook, The Weekenders, Beach Town, Save the Date, Ladies' Night, Christmas Bliss, Spring Fever, Summer Rental, The Fixer Upper, Deep Dish, Blue Christmas, Savannah Breeze, Hissy Fit, Little Bitty Lies,* and *Savannah Blues.* A former journalist for *The Atlanta Journal-Constitution,* she lives in Atlanta, Georgia.

The employees of Thorndike Press hope you have enjoyed this Large Print book. All our Thorndike, Wheeler, and Kennebec Large Print titles are designed for easy reading, and all our books are made to last. Other Thorndike Press Large Print books are available at your library, through selected bookstores, or directly from us.

For information about titles, please call:
(800) 223-1244

or visit our website at:
gale.com/thorndike

To share your comments, please write:
Publisher
Thorndike Press
10 Water St., Suite 310
Waterville, ME 04901